Alfred Vine

The doom of Saul and other poems

Alfred Vine

The doom of Saul and other poems

ISBN/EAN: 9783337206826

Printed in Europe, USA, Canada, Australia, Japan

Cover: Foto ©Andreas Hilbeck / pixelio.de

More available books at **www.hansebooks.com**

THE DOOM OF SAUL

(FRAGMENTS OF AN EPIC)

AND

OTHER POEMS

BY

ALFRED H. VINE.

LONDON :

HORACE MARSHALL & SON,

TEMPLE HOUSE, TEMPLE AVENUE,

AND

125, FLEET STREET, E.C.

1895.

CHATHAM:

W. & J. MACKAY & CO., "OBSERVER" WORKS.

To my Love
and Greatest Friend,
MY WIFE,
I Dedicate this Book.

From her dark mooring under the jetty
    Loose we our galley that strains with the tide,
Head for the harbour's luminous broadway,
    Halfway these tremulous shadows divide.

Sit you as captain holding the tiller :
    Docile our boat travels under the yoke,
Crosses alert the hill's dark reflection :—
    Midnight turned morning there at a stroke !

See high above us, burning intensely,
    Altars of seraphim, crest after crest ;
Now round the headland, steering her deftly,
    Mightily flashes the glory suppressed !

Dances the prow on a golden commotion,
    Under the stern there is blue *lazuli,*
Overhead flaunt imperial awnings,
    Amber and gold, all the clouds of the sky !

Beams of the sun and the sea aureole you,
    Crown you with jewels blown out of the west !
Frolic of hair, of ribbon and feather,
    Flutter of kerchief, and ruffle of vest,

Play of the boat that sways in the dazzle,
    Rush of the pinions of gulls that fly home,
Rapidly wheeling, darting, and curving,
    Wash of the water and curl of the foam—

All interpose with touches mesmeric,
    Veil and remove you from positive view ;
Set in a realm of sceptical fancy
    One whom aforetime so surely I knew.

Queen are you, sea born ? sea throned ? Or, rather,
    A dream-bird, joy-crested, loved of the sun ?
Poised there so lightly, will you take wing, then,
    Fly to some Arcady when the day's done ?—

See the brave Archer raining his gold shafts,
    Kindling the forest, and lighting the leaf !
Prodigal he this ultimate moment—
    Sped the last arrow of all the full sheaf !

So we pull homeward in a rich gloaming,
    Blossom and fruit of an apricot sky :
Calm now are winds and wings and the water—
    Calm too are you as the tiller you ply.

Are you a bird, or cerulean queen, love,
    Shimmering, fleeting, and cheating my life ?
Other, far better, this many a bright moon !—
    O you are my sweetheart, you are my wife !

Manchester, 1894.

CONTENTS.

CONTENTS.

THE DOOM OF SAUL

AND

OTHER POEMS.

THE DOOM OF SAUL.

THE COMING OF DAVID.

He came, as light might break at eventide ;
    Or spring in winter stir ;
Or fountain start in deserts wide ;
    Or far sail gleam to shipwrecked mariner.

And winter-prisoned hope came forth and laughed
    In his brave presence sunned ;
While sorrow now the spice-cup quaffed,
    That many a day her withered lips had shunned

He had the incommunicable grace
    That nature gives and God ;
A blended charm of soul and face—
    Unction of heaven and of the earth he trod.

The freedom of the wind—the verve of flame—
    A planetary calm—
The tenderness of clouds that frame
    The sun's decline—the rapture of a psalm

Breathed from the lips of day that wakes anew—
    And the sincerity
Of noontide's deepest farthest blue—
    Withal, betimes, midnight's austerity :—

These nature gave.   God gave the seer's eyes,
   And the son's loyal heart,
A soul to hear the harmonies
   Of heaven and earth, the part and counterpart,

And yet new harmonies to meditate,
   On a more perfect plan,
When comes, what earth and heaven await—
   And God himself—the full sweet song of Man.

———

A darkness fell upon King Saul, darkness
Disturbed by light—a quivering gloom, as when
A chariot's wheels revolve against the full
Clear moon that rises in a vale, and make
A throbbing shadow.   Pulsed thus doubtfully,
In rarer intervals, the better mind :
And less the good he would he did, and less
The bad he feared escaped, and more and more
His nobler purposes were disannulled,
Till the most settled laws of right were glossed ;
As by a foolish scribe a palimpsest
Is scrawled, in mere caprice, with other themes,
Or insolent, or sinister, or vile.
Treason against himself he wrought ; but men
The usurpation mourned without avail.
Th' apothecaries, rarely foiled in art,
Compared and then combined their lore in vain,
Their skill not having any mastery.
For neither aloe branches shrewdly placed,

Nor the dread hemlock strewn, nor frankincense,
Nor hellebore, nor red mandragora,
Nor the bright soothing asphodel, nor moly
White-blossoming, had virtue for the need.
For he forsook the converse of the house
And fell from all his kingly habitude,
Until men mused if ever Saul had been,
Who, fronting heaven with open brow, bore still
The signet of God's peace, in privacy,
In council chamber and in war : so raged
In passion-bursts, from room to room, or stalked
Abroad the stark yoke-fellow of the storm,
Or in presageful silence darkling fumed,
Another Saul, whom men knew not, nor could
Foresee.   The priest, and mighty man, and man
Of war, the ancient, and the counsellor,
With talk of the behoof of kings approached,—
Of custom, use and need ; or sought to cast,
As 'twere from invisible hands, the rein
Of soft dissuasives o'er him—health and peace,
Children by the throne, the lustre of his name—
Conjured him to resume his royal mood,
Nor let himself go drift, upon a wide and weary sea,
Into the night.   But at the last spake one,
Whose speech was slow and had a calmness in't,
Choosing the time—like as a woman seeks
To turn the edge of hardness in a man,
Just as the twilight falls— and " O my king,"
Said he, " not always can the swift stag run
His course ; nor always can the eagle soar ;

The wind will sleep sometimes on Lebanon ;
The sun his going down, the clearest moon
Her season knoweth ;—yea, and the vast world
Pauseth in labours prodigal, when fade
The flower and leaf, when russet fruits are stored,
And the dark vine-juice bubbles in the vat.
So thou, O king—the greatness of thy way
Hath wearied thee.   Yea, 'tis a noble thing,
To feel the task's nobility.   Heavy thy toil !
Nor wilt thou stay thine hand, while scattered wide
In all the cloudy and dark day of wrong,
The nation cries to thee for shepherding.
Yet solace must Saul have, though but a cup
Of water by the way—a cordial if
The spirit faint—war's harness just unlaced—
Then grip the bow and spear again !   And we,
Thy servants, have bethought how dear to thee
Is the sweet sound of lute or voice ; and God
Hath formed one for this ministry, a youth
All simple as the sheep he tends, but skilled
To play and sing, as sang the morning stars,
When God first made the great world's goodliness.
So that (men say) all trouble fleeth as
A dream, and we forget the face of foes,
The pain of wounds, our sorrow for the lost,
All jars of statecraft, and the cares that come
As birds that darkly fly across the fields,
When light is low, and grey is all the world :—
So soothes his song ; as when the body's bathed
Upon its weariness, and in soft linen lapped

While slumber lightly falls, mildly anoints,
Loosens each sinew strained, and smooths the flesh.
Thus from the bath of these sweet sounds, the mind
Emerges, and so rests awhile, till now,
Refreshed, she lifts her head again to see,
Shining in clearer air, the life's high prize.—
Thereto, the youth is wise, and hath a face
Fashioned as if to make men think of God."
So Saul sent messengers to Bethlehem
With royal mandate charged—" O Jesse, hail !
Thy son, the shepherd, let him come to me."
Him found they sitting on a bulk of rock
That jutted squarely from the curving hill,
Like ruined castle of the Nephilim.
On either side was half a league of slope,
Damasked with many flowers, red and blue,
That not alone the turf diversified,
But scaled the cliff, and hung their glowing fronds,
Banners of joy, from many a sullen crag.
And round the windy hill the white flock grazed,
Their fleeces blown back like a sea of foam :
But hence he led them, when the evening fell,
With harp strains, to the quiet fold.
       Now when
The archers came with summons from the king,
They looked to see in him rustic amaze,
Mingled with fear, to stand before great Saul.
But, after due obeisance made, he turned
On them a gaze so calm and clear, so fixed
Yet innocent, that less they wondered at

The morning beauty of the face they saw,
Than at the steady poise of mind unmoved.
And afterward would men this proverb say—
" That, whoso standeth oft before the Lord,
Shall have no need to quail before the king.
So David came and touched his magic harp,
And sang of the great order of the world,
Until the king's ears were attuned to hear
Long-hidden harmonies ; and obscured hopes
Revived, and he beheld himself once more
Upon the topmost crest of God's designs.—

Where are they now, who lifting up standards of battle,
Gath'ring assailed us in long succession of cohorts,
Rank on rank like the inexhaustible ocean,
When the tides gather full with the moon and the sundown ?
Now with a roar, and with myriad white plumes of onset,
Fierce flash the waves o'er outlying shingle and boulders,
Gleaming a moment against dark hollows of caverns,
Then beaten back in turmoil by the main cliffs opposing ;
Till the wide sea is blanched by the spume of the breakers.
Now comes the sunshine—gold once again on the headland !
See ! neither breach nor rent in the lofty embrasure ;
So from their dark haunts they swarmed in days that are past us,
—Edom and Moab proudly with Amalek banding ;
So they broke in their tumult, and vanished, pursued by
Laughter and scorn of the virgin, the daughter of Zion.

Ho ! from the north and the south come forth with your armies !
Yet shall ye be as the untimely fruit of a woman !
For God, yea, our own God shall help us, yea, save us right early !

Song.

When first my love confessed she loved
She spake not one melodious word;
  But with her eyes
  Said, "O arise
Sweetheart of mine, and be my lord."

I took her hand and touched her lips—
Of such a shining character,
  Love hath no need,
  The lore to read,
An audible interpreter.

So moved each heart to other then,
Ev'n as two dewdrops trembling near,
  By influence sweet,
  Each other greet,
And coalesce in one bright sphere.

Now oft in silence do we sit,
The flow of soul with soul to keep:
  For speech is yet
  A rivulet;
But silence is the boundless deep.

"'Tis true—not tall as some—not as a palm
 Or fir tree; but as an oak, or terebinth,

Whose height doth not surprise you, though the form
With strength and shapeliness the eye contents :—
While as a cedar grown upon the slopes
Of southern Lebanon our father seems.
For lo ! the sunlight strikes upon the crown,
And bathes the sweep of its dark emerald,
Yet rarely reaches to the inner gloom,
Flushing the central prop with tides of day.
Wherefore I made this song when David came :—
" The cedar stands alone for worship.   Sing
O maidens, sing Jehovah's right-hand plant !
And for your love O maidens choose the oak !
Sitting beneath, ye catch the blue of heaven,
And sifted glory through the golden leaves !"
So sang I to myself for many days,
Before that love had found the voice of love,
Or dared to own itself.
               I little thought
Such love could grow between us, at the first.
For when the tidings stole about the house
That one was come, a shepherd from the hills,
To soothe with harp the King's mind nigh distraught—
And in the fear that fell upon us,then
Hushed were all other sounds,—hearing the twang
Of strings I moving softly to the door
Through the disparted curtains saw the harp
Trembling, and then the hands supple and strong
That smote it, then at times the head bowed low
With waves of red-brown hair that caught the light
Glowing in all dishevelment.   The face

I could not fully see, or had not feared.
Ah, the harp! the voice! joining, following
Now one the other, into chords so sweet
That, unawares the heart was caught, and had
No will, and chose to have no will, but still
To fasten to the lips of sound.   He sang
Of birds, their nesting times, their brooding wings;
Of trees that grow so fair to God; of winds,
As angels from a country far that brought
Glad tidings; and of rivers with their streams
From founts of comfort flowing down.   But last
He sang of hills, and hollows, clouds and sky,
And turned it so, as if God bade the King
From peak to peak of great achievement move;
"Nor heed" he cried "the dragons crouched among
The rocks.   Or if *he* rise from his dark lair,
And thou must strive, as in the days of old
Fought Michael the archangel—*but thyself,*
Or prey or prize,—fear not my King! thy God
Shall then deliver thee! the heavens shall bend
In pity all their power! yea, though thou fall
In the fierce grapple for thy soul, fear not,
The dragon shall be under thee, O Saul."
At "under thee" I thought to see the harp
Flash fire, so mightily he struck the chords;
Then ceased, while his clear voice went on alone
Down sinking in the heart at the name "Saul."
    But when I heard the deep sighs of the King
As of a wounded man in pain who will
Not show his pain, I marvelled at the man

And his strange minstrelsy, as if he scarce
Were man.   Though, after, that voice spiritual,
Wrestling with all the demons of the air,
Brought comfort only, more familiar grown.—
Then once or twice in the broad vestibule
We chanced to meet—so that I knew him fair,
Serene, and gracious as a summer day,
But love—I scarce had thought of love a moon ago.
    That day returning mid the shout
Of a great multitude, the sound of horns
Drum-beat and cymbal, rain of flowers, he marched
With foot elastic as the roe's, yet firm.
We two were foremost in a bunch of maids
I' the open way :—I said to Merab, 'See,
His gait is as a prince's, fearing nought,
Yet asking eyes of none '—to pleasure her.
But ill content she seemed.   The deed I praised,
She answered carelessly—' O chance, belike.'
Then I : 'Such men and happy chances meet ! '
Whereat with sudden heat she flushed and frowned :—
' No happy chance that flings him thus on me.'
We ceased ; but in my heart I mused, 'this chance
Still hovers o'er with wing imperial,
And has not settled on its golden nest '—
(My bird, my phœnix of the sky and sun !)
Specially, too, because in passing he
Looked keenly on me, with so fixed a glance
As no one else were by.
                                        Not often had
We met, when on a day (O rainbow day !)

While as I lingered in the inner porch
That darkens to the court-yard, where the white
Light beats among the oleanders, he
Passing to audience, touched my hands and left
A lotus there, culled from some brimming pool.
O then I knew—

    And so it was that when
He sang at our espousals, how the moon
Was mated with the sun, and all the stars
Were damsels in her train—since love, he said
Was ever law in heaven, I, half ashamed,
Told him my song. A moment he perused
My face (nay —'tis as if he comes to you
Himself, searching and entering by his eyes.—
My father has a sapphire ring that seems
Quick with a spirit, so alive and clear
With darting tendernesses doth it shine.
But it is not so blue.) Then laughed a laugh
Joyous as spring, and caught me in his arms
And triply kissed.

    And so my tree is mine."

JONATHAN.

Song.

Make fast my heart to thine!
  For I shall need a friend
  At any day's dark end,
When stars forget to shine.
Make fast my heart to thine!

O set me as a seal
  Upon thine arm and heart!
  So last from me to part,
Though time all else shall steal!
O set me as a seal!

O be my convoy dear!
  For lone the wide sea is
  Between that life and this:
Thy signal flag shall cheer!
O be my convoy dear!

So might we haply gain
  At once the unknown strand!
  And there walk hand in hand:
Brothers at home remain—
If haply land we gain!

———

O blessed bondage of two equal men!
When each doth throne the other in his heart

Crowning him with his chiefest crown of love,
And serve him in that undisturbed domain
With oft-repeated ritual of praise ;
While mutual faith doth guard the doors without,
Lest Jealousy or Envy, liveried
As Truth—twin bastards of self-love—approach
To secret stab the heart's dear sovereign.
Blest such, as knowing they are worshipful
One to the other ; for so must either,
Being true-hearted, seek to be indeed
Such as his friend conceives, and by the cords
Of love, threefold, be ever drawn to be
Incorporate with that same nobleness ;
While on the baser self the mark of Cain
He sets.

Your forms, ye Twain, the troubled disc
Pass o'er of times and seasons long ago,
Softening the rude scene.   By storm and gloom
Pursued—the clouds high-toppling, underlapped
With thunder—do ye come in fearfulness :
But, whereso'er ye meet, God parts the clouds,
Letting a glory fall upon your heads.

From Naioth unto Gibeah of Saul
Fled David, as a deer hard-pressed turns home.
In a shy haunt by Ezel waited he
Through the vast hours of darkness for the day—
The day that broke with cloud on cloud, but low
In the East a rosebud light, that lingered—
Yet with the morn durst not break covert, lest

Night-woven meshes snare him, and the trees
And shrubs surprise, or dusky hollows teem
With sudden-crawling hirelings of the King.
          Now as the day grew blank he heard the‸whizz
Of arrows, and the voice of Jonathan
Call loudly to the lad that came with him—
" O further yet afield !   Beyond thee, boy !"—
The signal of their dark fears ratified !
Then in the heart of David died all light,
For now remained no other thing than this—
To wander forth alone through all the grey
And tedious years ; of noble fellowship
Bereft, despoiled of honour and of peace.
Wan grew the lips of Hope and could not speak.
But in a while, the lad dismissed with bow
And archer's gear, while Jonathan abode,
Wistful yet fearful, if that he might glean
Some token of his friend from shrouding bush
Or baffling rock, and so wave silently
A farewell from afar, David arose
In very Death's despite, and bowed himself
Before the prince.   Then either strong man wept,
And kissed the other in love's lavishment :
For now the great tide of time's circumstance
They saw divide their soul's communion :
Broken the intercourse of golden years !
Closed the inspiring vision each of each !
Sealed now the fountains of replenishment,
That yielded oft renewal of heart-ease,
Or filled the mind with truth once more

As from deep wells of wisdom.

      At the last
Spake Jonathan : " O brother we have sworn
By height and depth before the Lord ; nor time,
Nor chance, nor fate, compel disloyalty.
Therefore in my just thought of thee rest thou,
As in an embayed harbourage, where God
Makes smooth the waters with his breath—there float
Mild sea-birds, sailors sing, though all without
The grey scud hurries with the shrieking wind.
Thou too shall be my human haven dear.—
But for the rest, thou art not shelterless !
Wide as the world is that pavilion kind
Whose curtaining God draws round whom He loves.
I know God loves thee, friend. The print of grace
Was visibly expressed in all thy shape,
From sunlike head to thy winged feet, when first
I saw thee home-returning, victor-crowned.
God in thee then I knew: to thee, elect,
I saw the heavenly signature affixed.
No thanks to me, who did but note and say
" Praisèd be God "—what else ?—Between His choice
And man's review was no disseverance ;—
But God was justified in thee to all.
What if I noted the sign manual
Of God, with quicker eyes than some ? O this
Was my reward, that as a prophet I
Might freely herald it, the first of all—
And link myself for aye with God and thee :
For leagues of land and the long various years

     C

Can never now divorce our names : In thee
Shall I have honour, length of days, and God.
Yea—God at last ! when all the devious course
Is traversed, and the unknown close is reached,
Then shall a Face from out the dark greet mine,
Not unfamiliar, seeing I know thee.

Meanwhile in this entanglement of life
I have no skill to steer by any star
Save the one star of truth.   I follow this.
            But O my father !—darkly do I scan
Thy fateful way.   Stricken of God art thou,
And I in thee am stricken, as He wills !
Yet would He have me in thy westering path
Stand at thy side in offices of love,
To represent Him now awhile withdrawn.—
So may the smiting healing be at last !
Then I shall wind my arms about thee close
When He shall strike the final judgment stroke—
Of healing, father—and a little blunt
The sharpness ; and so pass to that dim goal,
Where doubtless doth some bright surprise await."

So murmured Jonathan grief-laden words.

Then looked they with exceeding steadfastness
In one another's eyes, until sorrow
Dislimnèd sorrow's self and blotted out
Their cognizance in tears.   Then with a low
"God keep thee, brother," either went his way.

AH, who may abide
The Day of His Coming ?
The Day of Consuming
   Who may abide ?
Who may behold Him
Vestured in purity ?
Who may security
   Find, if He chide ?

Who may confront Him
The Judge of the Ages ?
Who shall, life's pages
   Perusing, be bold ?
Who shall withstand Him ?
Raise up a mutiny ?
Question the scrutiny
   He shall unfold ?

Who may accuse Him
The Holy, the Equal ?
The verdict, the sequel
   Who shall dispute ?
If He condemn us
Our hearts will not clamour,
Our tongues will not stammer :—
   We shall be mute !

———

" The night is all thatched down with mirk : no star
  Glints out beneath the overhanging eaves

Of all the whole round roof of heaven !   Alas,
So hides He utterly from whom He set,
And published leader of the broken tribes,
By me to be compacted, disciplined
Into a front impregnable against
The aliens !   Such eminence I shunned :
Nor, with raw eagerness, as others, clutched
Some wandering chance—much less my footsteps hewed,
By craft and labour, in the risky steep
Throne-topped.   But all was as He would.   His hand
Propelled me from calm pastoral employ,
Who now degrades, makes abject before all.
Why, having led with hand peremptory,
And thrust into the thick of stratagems,
Flouts He my kingship, and constrains to crawl,
Leaving no inch where I may judgment use
Of what is fittest to the time, and new
Complexion of the thing ?   I, giving charge
To Abner, " Go on this emprize," do not
So straiten him in the command, but that
He shall be free to swerve from the strict line—
A little swerve—if that the end be reached :
Not only that a hundred things may hap
To change the prudence of the ways and means,
But that the man's soul be not manacled.
And if the bulk be gained, I trouble not
` For husk and dust of mere exactitude—
Though yet, at times, for policy, I say
That thus, and thus alone, a thing be done,
Fearing men fail in reverence for the King.

But Him no fear of questioned rule assails.
Yet, lo ! in nicest balances He weighs
To me, me Saul, my task a tale of work—
Bids me give curious heed to note, amid
The stormy plunder of a cursèd tribe,
The scruple less or more of done—not done.
Thus curbs me with minute restrictiveness,
As lion in the hunter's pit and net,
What time the winter hunger makes him fain.

    Crossed were the trivial bounds : yet heedfully—
With reason, I allege.   But He marks not.

    And when I knew that He was wroth with me,
Did I stint sacrifice ?   Nay, to repair
The flaws in my obedience, I searched
How I might serve Him with excess ; so set
Free homage on the counter side : for this,
Have I lain prostrate, bare on the bare ground,
The livelong night, beneath the astonished stars.
But He marks not.   His prophets have I sought,
Bidding them use their utmost arts to learn
The secret of propitiation—scan
The Urim for the light I need—omit
No nicety of worship, or of rite.
Thus would I, crouching, make amends for all,
Softly attend Him.   But He marks me not :
Silent He passes on His mighty way,
Deaf to all pleas, disdainfully averse.
More than the captive craves for his release,
More than the mourner watches for the morn,
More than the lover longeth for the bride,

Long I, in this prodigious void of life,
This wide distended dumbness of the heavens,
Swelling with judgment, for the voice of God.—
    Speak, though Thou curse me, and Thy cursing rives
My soul as lightning rives the oak—yet speak !
Speak Holy One !   Thou God of Samuel !
Thou Lord and God of David hear Thy Saul !
(Alas Thy David is it, not Thy Saul !)
    If yet He will not hear in this extreme,
And there be ways, ways of the dusk and stealth,
By which a King may haply gain access,
And secret hear—what harm in secrecy ?—
The undivulged decree of heaven, though with
Increase of doom ; then would I rather bear
The charge and surcharge of law's strictest mulct,
Than so, in common, grossest ignorance,
Writhe like a wretched blind-worm in the dark."

Thus in the darkness ruminating stood
King Saul, and with an evil industry
The mesh of falsehood spread to catch his soul ;
Then doffed his Royal raiment, and in cloak
Sordid and unemblazoned, wrapped his form,
The towering helmet on his grizzled locks
Replaced by leathern cap, a naked sword,
Ready for sudden deed, in his right hand.
So fared forth stooping, shrunken, vigilant,
With foot of fox threading Philistia's camp
All unalert, and heard the midnight shout
Of thunder as of captains in the heavens,

And the swish of a great rain resounding,
As when the rapid whips of charioteers
Are plied in onset—heard and feared, and yet
Return more feared :—so moodily passed on,
To seek mid bowers of hemlock and henbane,
The witch, with puckered face and parchèd skin,
As of brown lizard, who at Endor dwelt,
Fatal in ancient story, and there wrought
Her worst in spells, in charms, and devilry.

ENDOR.

1.

ALL the kind stars are gone
    To the last spark!
Wind and the wave roll on
    Together—Hark!
To their unison dread,
As they cry underneath, overhead!

2.

Captain, what of the night—
    This night so dark?
Dost thou sail in despite
    Of heaven thy bark
In the fell hurricane?
Canst thou hope the far haven to gain?

3.

Who, sailor, thee shall save?
    Thine is no ark
Plunging through the black wave
    Toward God's mark!—
See the ship falls a wreck,
And thy pilot lies dead on the deck!

4.

On to the mid-sea rock
  See the boat drifts!
Where the great tidal shock
  Seething uplifts
A white passion of foam,
Thou dost find—is it God? is it home?

———

A sound as of a thousand brazen thrones
Falling down endless chasms in the hills
Brake from the skies, and clanged with echoes long
From shore to shore, region to region far,
Then murm'ring failed from the extremest sense,
And heaven and earth were soundless as the deep
Below the deep of the wide sea; when Saul—
Ev'n as a stag sore wounded swaying turns
To sniff the scent of flushed hounds following,
Then totters to the thicket to lie down,
Until the hunter's final horn arouse—
One moment on the ridge of Shunem stood,
With strained glance looking southward wavering,
Adread, forespent, and full of mighty care;
Yet not so careful of life's better part,
As now to grasp at its retreating clue,
And hold to it through darkness and through all.
Then gat he down the hill, nor turned again;
But with his servants wearily went on,
Until he stumbled o'er a barren slope,
Leprous with stones innumerable, scaled

From the cliff by the winter frost and rain,
And found beneath a shelf of lichened rock
A hollow in the hill, and thence a cave. Hard by
A cypress grew and spindling tamarisk,
Root-bridled by the ruck of cromlech stones
That prone, or stand, or upright, round the lair
Confused the door. Here in recesses dank
Throve poison-shrubs with sullen purple bells,
Long-stalked tway-blossomed plants that looked askance,
All sallow as the belly of a snake,
With many a far-brought livid herb and thorn
And blotchy weed, with foul dew glistering.

One small lamp burning at the cave's far end,
Now entering from the pitchy night, they saw
Cast fitful glimmer on the garniture
Of hateful things upon the roof and walls
And rocky floor—unheard of efts with huge
Distended gills and horns, and creatures squab,
Misshapen, misbegotten—or alive
Or mummied, or in images. Here dwelt
A sorceress of Canaanitish race,
In whose veins ran the ichor of false gods :—
So old she was it seemed that wearing time
Had ceased to vex her with his changes more,
And men lost record of the years she lived,
Whom fathers' fathers wondered at and feared.
Upon her wrist she wore an asp encurled,
That looked a stone until it blinked an eye
More stony than a stone ; and a long robe

Of ancient purple mixed her, as she moved,
With shadows, save her face that peaked and grey
Showed as a meteor in a misty sky.
Wily she was and sinuous as a snake,
Winding round all supposed forbidden things,
Not having honest zeal to know, and in
That zeal knowing no difference between
Clean and unclean, if only might be grasped
The whole of truth ; but lusting after power
Through knowledge sinister, conceived apart
From God ; and so familiarly to ply
Whatever bane or bale nature exudes
In form or essence.   Deemed herself a queen
In the realm partial, several, obscure
Where truth dips down through twilight to the deep,
That God sees ; but a slave far rather was
To phantoms and chimeras of the mind.

   Now when the hooded King advanced, with mind
Razed blank of gracious records, furrowed o'er
With fears, and craved an audience with the dead,
In that great loneliness that now was his,
The witch screamed, as the white sea-osprey screams,
When a bold cragsman reaches overhead
His hand to search her eyrie perilous.
But when her fear was pacified, she wrought
By many arts to fall into a trance.
Now at the cavern's uttermost, the floor
Brake into depth no plummet ever reached ;
And at the brink she kindled incense, thick
With resinous gums and drugs, whereof the smoke

In fluent lines drew upward to a spire,
While all the cave was filled with heady fume:
Next stooped and cried aloud into the depth,
Invoking the dead Samuel, and far
The hollow sound re-echoed underneath.
Now the smoke trembled o'er the pit in swaths,
Wavered in curls, gathered in draperies,
Or drawn by gentle currents nimbly moved
Inquiringly into each murky nook.
And still she crooned, and called on Samuel;
And still the blue smoke wavered into forms,
Whatever fancy pleased, or frenzy wished:
Until deceiving, and not less deceived,
She half believed, and wholly claimed she saw
The seer late passed into the peace of God—
Not now to be disturbed in that serene.
Then she not ignorant of policies
And cunning in the chances of the time,
As sailors in the changes of the wind,
With ventriloquial voice oracular
Gurgled forth forecasts of the coming fight,
While the lorn King was yielded to her will.
As a scared child in panic questions not
The words of ghostly terror nurses tell,
But greedily drinks down into his soul
All the dark fear; so Saul undoubting heard
Each fearful syllable that sealed his doom,
Until he lost himself in dread, nor heard,
Nor saw, but seemed to wander evermore
In a dark avenue, dipping to the west,

Hastening to follow Samuel who fled.
And when he caught him by his raiment's wings
Lo it was David with an angel's face !
Then darkness utter, and no face at all,
Nor David's, Samuel's, nor Jonathan's ;
But in the dim path wildly still he went,
Cursing the sun gone down, asking for light—
Demanding light as God—" Let there be light "—
Or sobbing for it as one dungeon-held,
Who knows that light and he have said farewell.
So stumbled into vacancy.

                The witch,
When she beheld the King thus desperate
And utterly foredone, was moved with fear,
Yea, and some pulses of the mother stirred
In her long withered breast, and ruth prevailed
To see him stretched as dead upon the ground,
Like a great column broken from its base.
Then raised they up the wan man tenderly,
Constraining him to eat awhile the bread
Of sorrow.

      So departing ere the dawn,
Saul saw great Tabor's peak at length divide
The clouds, and in the rifts and high above
Ages of depths, powdered with stars so fair
And far, and, as a ghost, the withered moon.

DAVID'S LAMENT.

ONE night the bare dark ground of my sleep
  Yielded a milk-white bloom
That grew to a world, where clothed with the light
  One sat at a mighty loom.

High as the heavens the canvas rose,
  Wide as the poles its span :—
And I knew that the weaver sitting there
  Was weaving the life of man.

But dimly the weaver's work I saw :
  Blurred was the wondrous scheme :
Too vast was the scale for my human eyes :
  Too bright the heavenly beam.

Then He, who wrought the picture rare,
  Spake to me soft and low,
As the voice of infinite forest trees,
  When the west winds come and go.

"One moment thou may'st stand by my side
  And see as angels see,
And view in my light what I do for men—
  The light of Eternity."

Then I saw He held all mortal threads
  In colours manifold ;
But ever there ran with each single strand
  A thread of sun-bright gold.

The moment passed as I heard His voice :
  " Time's web in love began !
And the golden thread that thou seest is
  The pity I have for man."

        ———

So David sat within the house and wept
For Saul and Jonathan.   Before him lay
On the divàn the dead King's coronet
Brought by the false Amalekite, and torn
From the helm ; the gold armlet all embossed
And centred with a spheric jasper stone.
These mournfully regarding, David sighed :—
" Poor relics of thy Beauty, Israèl !
How oft this circlet blazed above war's press !
This jewel flashed at stroke of the strong arm,
Now nevermore to be uplift upon
God's enemies and ours !   A bulwark thou,
O Saul, stood'st in this land through evil days,
When, like the growing tide still sucking force
From half-spent waves, the bands of Philistines
From Aroer and Gaza fiercely rolled,
Unto Jezreel : Yet thou undaunted drew,
Uniting by thy sole heroic mind,
The baffled units of our race, the weak,
Witless or desperate, and made them strong;
Nay, in the course of discipline and law,
Thou didst lay sure the stones of settled rule
For after days, which God shall bring to pass.
Not fruitless then thy life !—Ah, who shall say,
When the dread gates of Sheol yawn for all,

That God hath had due vintage year by year,
Harvest of field and flock, no plot untilled,
Of all the fair estate he lent to each ?
For with the sun man goeth forth jocund
Unto life's work ; but wearies when his day
Declines.   So thou, my king !—Yea mine !—This joy
I have to-day, that never did I lift
Or hand or voice against thee, in the years
When thou wast other than thyself :   .
Nor could forget how thou, magnanimous,
Did'st call me from the shade of shepherd life
Into the glory of thy own ; nor yet
With treasonable thought did dare to guess
How other things, heaven-willed, should come to be ;
Or sought with artifices fine the least
Enforcement of the providential plan.
For when God said to me—I knew not why—
"Thou shalt be King"—I knew not how—did I
Pluck branch, or leaf awry, that suns and moons
Might earlier purple this my prize ?   God said,
"The cluster is for thee" : the fruit was green :
Yet did I, ev'n in fancy ripen it ?
Not so, my dread dead father-king !

                                   If aught
Thou knowest now of miserable years,
When thou didst walk bewildered and amazed ;
As shepherds whom the mountain mist involves,
While seeking ewe or lamb astray, mis-judge
Of path and rock and haggard tree—and crags
Immediate at the feet breaking divide,

By sword-edge, life from death :—to thee my mind—
If aught thou knowest—will now show as clear,
And constant firm, as the white crystal is.
(Not always seen in those sad wandering years).
Phantoms thou sawest : I a phantom seemed
Amid the abhorrent gloom. But thou, lost friend !—
God keeps my memory unvexed and sweet
For thee, and Jonathan !—O thou, twin soul
Of mine, whose truth was as the truth of God,
Heart-bound to me for many noble years,
Wherein we walked with equal steps of love !—
Nay, I but strove to equal thee, who lost,
In the great splendour of thy love, thyself !
For thou, as herald, with unjealous mind,
Went still before me to make sure my way,
Chode with my love pursuing, gently waived
My claim to leadership in sacrifice,
Outvoiced me when I would demur, refused,
While turning the popular eye to me,
To be conjoined or measured with me, though
So easily surpassing ; trumpeting—
" What think ye of David ? David stands alone !
No one like David !"—No one like thyself,
Brother of my heart, loving me in God,
With flames that many waters could not quench !
    I hold you both in my remembrance set,
As in a silver mirror fair—could hand
But fix what there we do behold. No change,
No chance, the calm and settled sphere shall dim,
Where I shall see your lustrous images,

D

To me as pictures of the Sons of God,
August as those our great forefathers knew,
While yet the earth was green, nor hum of towns
And cities filled the land, and great sin came.
    Nor should I ever know, though length of days
As the hoar mountains were accorded me,
And sight of many nations, men so strong,
Excelling, swift, and beautiful as ye.

Lo I will make a song for men to sing
In after times, when war is at the gates
Hoarse-shouting, with the clash of myriad shields,
The fearful glancing of bright spears—when hearts
Do droop to see the rings of warfare drawn
Closer and closer, like the coils of snakes
That crush.   Then shall my song enhearten men
As with new wine, bring noble shame and wrath,
And Saul and Jonathan shall live again
In rally-cry and victory :—if God
Shall help me sing ; to whom, Eternal One,
My heart as incense shall for ever rise !"

THE MONTHS.

JANUARY'S EXPECTATION.

Not yet the blackthorn, through the dark
  Of hedgerows, makes a "milky way;"
Nor bleats the lamb; nor sings the lark
  His orisons at break of day.

A silent shadow in the thorn,
  The thrush with bright eye ponders still :—
And yet we are not all forlorn :
  The trees that grow on plain and hill

Etch the dun sky : in pools serene,
  Made by the high banks' curvature,
Their reflex exquisite is seen,
  In pensive, pensile portraiture.

In calm nooks some dear violet
  Will come to bless, in cold's despite:
And sculptured snowdrops, shrewdly set
  By grave and guardian trees, delight.

The maple-shoots are red with hope :
  The yellow wands of willows glow :
And chestnuts cast May's horoscope,
  With buds for stars, above the snow.

Tokens how faint are these !—a shred
  Of purple lurking in the moss,
A glint of white, a stain of red ;
  A fresher tint, a newer gloss—

And lo ! Spring's pursuivants we greet !
  And watch the New Year's opening door,
What time shall issue thence the sweet,
  Long train of living things once more.

A FEBRUARY NIGHT.

High are the clouds, enmeshed together;
   From far and near the north wind's fret
Has caught them—every floss and feather—
   Tangled them in a pearl-grey net.

Looks from a momentary chamber,
   Behind her curtains and thin veils,
The clear moon, showing locks of amber;
   Then shyly hides and softly sails.

How fair the time! What fancies waken!
   To lightly rove, by fear unvext,
As twilight moths, when dew is shaken
   From one full flower, will seek the next.

Say, here's a sea with billows hoary,
   This sky, whose motion never ceases;
Or, here's a plain, as in old story,
   Where clouds are flocks with snowy fleeces;

Or, here's a dreamland Argosy
   Crowding all sail for port unknown;
Or, wrought by Dian's poesy,
   A garden, with white lilies strown;

Or, here's a silver dome, whose circle
    The bound of all the world doth seem,
Far up the vaulting diamonds sparkle,
    Bosses of pearl and ivory gleam.

God's House is here ! Let this thought hold me !
    That roof of cloud, this floor of sod,
The faithful mountains that enfold me,
    Are His ! Come, let us worship God !

ALL heaven looks down with serious face
  Upon our little world beneath;
Yet are the dun clouds touched with grace
  Far in the east where fades the heath—

The heath that surges rank and brown
  Round yonder pillar of old days,
Then passes softly, dimly down,
  To lose itself in silver haze.

From the brown gloom the boulder springs;
  The eastern sky is fair to see;
The rock a sign of former things;
  The morning lights of things to be.

Alone on this wide heathery land,
  No other rock save this appears,
Hewn, carved by elemental hands,
  Here resting through millennial years.

Wrought was it at the primal source
  Of fire, in wrinkled nature's youth;
Hurled outward by some earthquake's force;
  Ground by the glacier's restless tooth,

Dark secret of some iceberg's breast,
    Floated from north or southern pole ;
Through warmer waters slipped to rest,
    Poised now upon this English knoll ;

Starred like a veteran after wars ;
    Rosettes of lichen and green moss
Crowd thick to beautify the scars,
    And tenderly transfigure loss.

With yellowing stream yon light is flowing ;
    We taste the March wind's cheerful zest ;
Soon will a world of wild flowers blowing,
    Yield smell of fields that God hath blest.

Maintain, O friend ! the wintry fight ;
    " The spring comes slowly up this way ;"
But turn, and face the unfolding light,
    " Until the shadows flee away !"

AN APRIL EVENING.

LATE music falls, in moan or trill,
　　From heights the haunt of bird and breeze
And o'er the clover rises still
　　A mist of murmurs from the bees.

A sea of grass flows in the vale :
　　Red uplands trenched so far and true
Glow in the sun : above clouds sail
　　In unpolluted depths of blue.

A wild stream runs amid the green,
　　And alder trees pursue its mazes :
Far off a heron, fisher keen,
　　With side-bent head intently gazes.

Soft clouds, the fitful zephyr brings,
　　Linger above yon western wold,
Like brooding doves with silver wings,
　　And burnished breasts of yellow gold.

Towards their sphere the wild swan made
　　Her own proud way, with dauntless carriage ;
Now level bends her course, afraid
　　That their bright plumes would her's disparage.

Scarlet as poppies are, the sun
  Sinks under clouds—triumphal arches,
Stained with the hue of roses wan,
  The grey of pearls, the green of larches.

From the tall tor the raven glides
  Into the vale, where something stirs :
Engraved above the mountain sides,
  Far up in heaven, dark files of firs.

This April day is now far spent,—
  As when those two delayed with prayers
And entertained, with wonderment,
  Indeed an Angel unawares.

God walks and talks with us through hours
  Of light, and life in myriad kinds:
His Face is in the clouds and flowers;
  His Voice is in the birds and winds.

That Face have ye not seen? nor heard
  Aught save the tones impersonal
Of the fair present life ? no word
  Of fuller life reversional ?

The day is done.   'Tis ours that life !
  Won out of bitter night and death ;
He lives the Victor in the strife ;
  " Ye shall live too," the Master saith.

WILD hyacinths, their deep blue waves
    With foam of wind-flowers flecked, fill now
The copse: the tide of colour laves
    Each stem, each winter-fallen bough,

Flows into hollows, floods the dikes,
    Scales every hillock's breast and crest,
Surges among the close-set spikes
    Of brier and bramble. Let us rest

Beneath this golden-tufted oak,
    And from our scented hermitage
View the bright scene. The care, the yoke,
    The doubt of life's strange pilgrimage

Pass all away. Just now a bird,
    From some last, finest, aspen spray,
Sang to the angels, and was heard :
    We could not choose but join his lay.

Before us soars a fir-clad ridge,
    And through the golden interspace
Their silver-weft dart fly and midge
    Like myriad shuttles weaving lace,

The wood-dove gurgles melody ;
  The field-mouse strays from her smal fold ;
The young lambs dream in Arcady ;
  The cattle couch on marigold.

We do not merely live to-day,
  We move in life, an element,
An ocean stretching every way,
  That knows no term or continent.

From shore to shore sweet voices calling,
  Tell us that Life, not Death, shall reign ;
But from the heavens One Voice is falling :
  " Ye enter *into* Life."   Amen !

JUNE ROSES.

THE rain fell yester eve, and brimmed
    All founts and springs. No cloud or gauze
Or haze this morning's lustre dimmed !
    Northward the sea, a pale turquoise ;

And then the ships : far off the shaft
    Of a forsaken rainbow, red
I' the offing, like a burning raft :—
    The angels built thus far and stayed

At sea mist level. Picturesque,
    Tall palisades of thorns and roses
Shadow our lane with arabesque :
    A rambling limestone cliff opposes,

That with an orderly disorder,
    Keeping a line it often ruptures,
Adorns with grassy coigns its border,
    With columns, shrines, recesses, sculptures ;

So runs far southward.—Fair the day,
    Wherein all trees and plants lift up
Themselves, to court the sun's clear ray,
    From oak to lowly buttercup.

But these wild roses waving free,
    Frail stars on sprays of chrysolite,
That fire the hedgerows to the sea,
    Are the delightful day's delight !

The frail stars dance, and opening buds
    Their kisses to the swallows throw,
Whilst breezes move, and odour floods
    The bowered path by which we go.

Take but one bloom within your hand—
    How frank and pure !   How free, and yet
In what symmetric measures planned
    From petal tip to coronet !

Freedom by truth is still endeared ;
    Obedience knows no prison bars ;
Beauty and law, in this small sphere,
    Glass the world's circle and the stars !

For thus the tide of being flows
    In rhythmic sweep, to every part :
The universe is God's great Rose,
    And Love its central golden heart !

JULY: THE NOON OF THE YEAR.

In mighty domes of oak and elm,
   In crimson and in purple flower,
In the bright life that throngs her realm,
   Nature attains her perfect hour!

Not more of life can she contain,
   Nor more of joy! no whispers rude
Of life that ebbs, of joys that wane,
   Disturb the quiet of her mood.

All harmonies around her wait;
   Upon her head the crown is set:
She pauses at her perfect state,
   To point to things not seen as yet.

Yet Beauty's guerdon is half pain,
   The while she hints the pure ideal;
And we recall the transient reign
   Of all this gracious unreal real;

And feel the lack, in part or whole,
   In us of correspondence true,
As to the form of our own soul,
   With the round world so fair to view;

Much more with what shall be, when forth
    All hidden founts of light shall stream,
And West and East, and South and North,
    Reveal the New Jerusalem.

Ah, tidings from a country far,
    Are these fair things thou seest and hast!
They voices of the herald are;
    But Christ Himself will come at last!

AUGUST AMONG THE HILLS.

CLIMB, comrade, where the sun's last beams
   Upon the mountain's crest of sod
Make a strange fire—climb till there seems
   Nothing between us men and God !

The young sheep bleat at our advance ;
   With anxious cry across the heather,
The grouse whirr like a flying lance ;
   Then silence, as we climb together.

Raised on the shoulders of the world
   Thrust into heaven, at last we stand :
Below, the vale in mist impearled ;
   Around, the purple wan moorland ;

Above, the amazing height of clear,
   Auroral crystal, like a gem
Wrought for pure joy :—yet have we here
   Only His lustrous garment's hem !

Nothing between us men and Thee ?
   Ah, easy, idle word to say !—
If this were Peni-el, and we
   Did wrestle all the night away !

E

Yet if He came at morning's prime
    And showed—the last veil drawn aside-
His Face, in majesty sublime,
    Then O my soul, couldst thou abide.

Yea, I would see Him !   But I need
    Some human Friend, and Friend divine,
To take my trembling hand, and plead—
    " Lo He is Mine, as I am Thine ! "

See how the stars their promise send—
    A Jacob's ladder faith can trace !
Darkling we know Him now, O Friend !
    But soon shall see Him face to face !

SEPTEMBER.

An Eastern Legend.

When Adam quitted Paradise,
    He came not empty-handed forth,
Old legend saith. The Lord All-wise
    Gave him three things of priceless worth:

Corn to afford him needful food—
    Then, added gracious overplus,
To fill him with a sense of good—
    The myrtle, shapely, odorous,

With scented star-cluster, and leaf,
    And the sweet date good cheer to yield:
These in their seeds,—vast wealth in brief,—
    Then sent him forth to till the field.

For this our life, that God designed,
    Was not mere life, shut in small round;
But liberal, adorned, refined,
    With joy of all the senses crowned.

Is not a flower pure gladness? Fruit
    Pure grace? God's cup runs over here—
The apple thy fond palm to suit—
    The rose that breathes of Eden dear.

E 2

But, say you, that by toil severe
　　Man from the waste his goods evoked?
That he compelled the desert drear,
　　By skill and labour duly yoked,

To show him hidden things, and thus
　　Secured contentment of his needs,
And gained the happy overplus?
　　Then say, O mortal! *whence the seeds?*

The world's fair possibilities,
　　Maintained in order permanent—
Its kindly plastic qualities?
　　Man's tastes and powers consonant?

The mutual law was plain.　God said
　　To man: "Go, in My vineyard toil!"
And to the world around him spread,
　　" Bring forth the corn and wine and oil! "

OCTOBER WOODS.

WALK in these rich paths while you may !
   The leaf that loiters from the bough
And, like a butterfly at play,
   Alights capriciously—e'en now !—

Leaves yet a myriad of his mates,
   That glow on branch and airy crest,
And break the azure of heaven's gates,
   With fervours caught from East or West.

Take while you may these hours serene !
   Deep unto deep of musing calls !
The dew that curves the sedges green
   Pauses long moments ere it falls !

Soon will wild winds and pouring floods
   Conclude the sylvan holiday,
Tear all the splendour from the woods,
   And cast the gold brocade away.

And Proserpine, her straying tresses
   Looped in her coif, no more will roam ;
But, turning from the sun's caresses,
   With wan face seek her dusky home :

Wild Winter like a prophet pass,
  Crying aloud from shore to shore :
" All glory dies ; all flesh is grass "—
  And breathe upon the mountain's hoar,

And on the valleys at their feet,
  And blur the light, and dim the sheen,
To make the parable complete—
  All goodliness, save God's, is vain.

NOVEMBER.

CONWAY CASTLE: A LUNAR RAINBOW.

DARK grey the sea ! Light grey the cloud !
    Vague moonshine touches shore and field :
Those towers, sky-framed, rise grim and proud,
    Bar sinister on silver shield.

The high tide runs its mighty race ;
    The wind roars from its western cave ;
The parted cloud-pack flies apace ;
    The moist stars blink beyond the wave ;

A diamond rain-dust fills the air,
    Mixed with the rheum of moony spray ;—
Who would not call the season fair ?
    Or who would wish November May ?

Rising behind those towers behold,
    Traced on the dim brows of the night,
Meek, clear, as timid and yet bold,
    The mighty curve of lunar light !

How soft yet sure its footsteps are,
    While passing to its perfect form,
From cloud to cloud, from star to star,
    Amid the bluster of the storm !

Mystic this silver yoke that weds
    The land and sea, and arches ships,
The town, the hills, our humbled heads,
    And in the wild Atlantic dips

Its foot far venturing!   The span
    Of Mercy and of Power is here,
That stretches o'er the life of man,
    And clasps the courses of the year.

DECEMBER. NORTH WALES.

THE Zephyrs breath was debonair,
   And rich with balm of bloom and bud ;
But this north wind is crisp and rare,
   And stirs the manhood in our blood.

Ah you regret the iris flown
   From the wide sea's circumference !—
Yet soft this misty monotone !
   Prize we the season's difference.

The hills were scarce more fair in May,
   When rainbows nestled there to dream :—
O'er that dim world beyond the bay
   A hundred peaks of opal gleam !

(So o'er the earthborn mists of time
   The citadels of Zion rise,
For ever rise in Faith's clear clime,
   Far in the land of Paradise !)

You sigh for mellow moons !   But mark
   God's compensation in the stars—
The keener light—the darker dark !—
   Latticed by summer's silver bars

Less brightly shone the starry train,
  To whom he metes the great profound :
Now on a burning throne they reign,
  Their purple empire sweeping round.

The jewel of the world God turns,
  And sets diverse in Love's clear ray ;
And in that gracious light it burns
  With some new facet every day.

BALAAM'S DREAM.

PREFATORY NOTE.

Several commentators consider that the terms used
imply that Balaam did not meet with his death in the
battle of the Kings; but received judicial sentence afterwards. It is on this supposition that the poem is founded.

I.

BALAAM'S DREAM.

Now pealed the silver trumpets of the hosts
Of God, keenly and long —sword blades of sound,
And thrusting spears !—till each man's heart was stung,
And like a winter lion leapt to win
The prey. So grasped they brand and shield,
And mustered in Beth-jesimoth at morn.

From Heshbon rolled the foes confederate,
From Ramoth, Rabbah, Ar and Kir, the tents
Of distant Kedar, Eneglaim steep,
Renamed in later time Callirrhoë ;
While from Nebaioth's hills, and Petra's caves,
Streamed forth allies who worshippèd The Shame.

Then, round the standards of their Gods unclean,
Fought Evi, Hur and Reba, Zur the Rock,
And Rekem broidered chieftain, fought and fell,
With many a captain of wild desert men,
Their crimson mantles dyed anew, their moons
Of gold all blurred with gory dust.   But some
Fled on their dromedaries to the waste :
And more, amid the thorny tanglement
Of the acacia groves, quaking, lay hid,
Till the blue Hebrew spears searched their retreat,
And the last gurgling prayer to Bel went out
In blood.   But when the men of Israël
Returned at trumpet call, they saw afar
A man uprising from a heap of slain,
As if awaking from a swoon, and would
Have killed.   Then Phinehas beholding him,
And taking note of golden stars and signs,
Inwrought upon the purple of his robe,
And mystic figures running round the hem,
Bade spare.   Him, therefore, bound with sheep-skin thongs
They brought into the camp, guarding till day.

And now the sun his broad and glowing seal
Beneath the day's full record set, and night
And dew and balm and starlight came.   Now slept
Archer and spearman in the dusky tents
That couched like some vast herd of creatures strange
Browsing in fairy-land at witching hour—
Dark all, save that, midmost, the Holy Place
Glowed like a chrysolite.

And Balaam slept,
And dreamed.   He saw himself return alone
O'er the red desert on a milk-white ass.
The wind was mourning on the plain, and puffed
The scuffled sand into a fume.   Behind,
From far, and craning east, stretched a vast cloud,
Black like a cormorant.   Then turning round,
Fearful he saw the hoof-prints of the ass
Brimming with blood, and far off in the west,
Storm cinctured, a bright-armoured angel set
In his pursuit, with brandished sword that swept
From North to South in a great arc of sheen.
Madly he fled, and blindly urged the beast
Till at the last, amazed, he now had reached
The aloe-scented shore of the great stream,
Whose broad expanse a magic mirror was,
Aforetime, to give images to thought.
There he alighting scarce three paces took,
Soothing himself and saying "all is well,"
When suddenly he saw before him one
Shrivelled and twisted like a desert shrub,
Who cried, " Hail to thee son of Beor !   Lo !
I bring a summons from the utmost sea "—
So drew forth from a hollow reed he bore
A scroll.   But Balaam, as he read perplexed,
Heard a vast sound, and lifting up his eyes,
Behold, the sea came everywhere,
And caught him in its toils, and wrapping round
With surges, even to the soul, dissolved him,
And mixed him with the deep : Then sinking far

Time's course passed over him unmarked, until
Arising as a solitary wave,
On a long shore, he rolled far inland, swept
The vineyards and the folds and stood at length
Poised, for a moment, over Midian's tents,
Then crashed, and crashing woke—

And lo the day !

II

BALAAM'S APOLOGY.

Ere yet the day's flower had unfurled full gold,
They brought him where, beneath the clustered palms,
The elders sat, and Moses in their midst,
Who, seeing Balaam as a felon bound,
Straightway commanded them to cut the thongs,
That he might stand before them unashamed.
So in his princeliness he stood erect,
And all men knew him who he was, though reft
Of followers, and turbanless, with smirch
Of battle on his robes.   His royal head
The neck columnar crowned—exquisite poise !
His long black hair, touched here and there with thought,
Tent-like divided from the brows divine ;
And in the arches shone the eyes as bright
As moonlit summer lakes ; while the round lips
Were like a maid's, disparting graciously.
Yet something of the satyr in the face,
And in the nostrils something of the hawk,
And something of the serpent in the mouth,
Confused the happier view.   For God at first
Had put a lustre as of morning clouds,
What time the sun has risen o'er the hills,

Upon his face ; nor was there any one
Anointed thus, with such a chrism of light,
Save Moses only ; but the pride of will,
And many subtleties, and mournful years,
Had made the glory wan, and dulled the sign :
And men, regarding him, perceived with awe
An angel had been there, and gone away.
Then Moses with exceeding calmness said,
" Speak Balaam, son of Beor, if thou wilt.
For thou art known : God's mark of greatness must
Be thy betrayal, if nought else : for loath
Are we to cut thee off like a dumb beast,
As if denying thy mere human rights ;
Or eager to foreclose revenge, afraid
Thy plea might snatch from us the prey.
Take to thee words, and ease thee of thy load,
Too vast, I deem, for one to bear alone."
But Balaam coldly answered : " Do ye ask
The bird to sing a song within the snare ?"
Then Moses said : " Thou knowest otherwise :
I will not cast upon thee what I might :
But—for thy soul—make God a partner—yea
And us, bearing thy injuries : So then
It may be all His anger will drain out
In this event, and death be life to thee."
Then musing silent for a little space
He answered : " Death be life ! Ah, can'st thou say ?
I see before me Death's dark door—but life !
Hast thou then looked within ?—Thy lips are locked
As God's ! So scarcely do I hope to gain

Your mirage-goal ; but I am inly urged,
Perhaps by vanity, perhaps by God,
To say what else were hid, though thou art wise
And thy clear eyes are like the stars that see
In darkness. As for these, they will, I think,
But understand in part ; nothing excuse :
So to the prophet let the prophet speak,
And others gather what they list or can.
Ye have but seen the crude result—fruit plucked
Half-ripe ; but I have writ a chronicle
To show some things I did in your behalf.
'Tis true I erred (as who may not ?) when first
The Son of Zippor called : yet afterwards,
Reproved, in that first business which ye know
In brief, I did not swerve from your desires ;
As ye shall read hereafter in the book.
But now, think ye, too grossly have I sinned :—
As if the way of truth were one plain track
Cut in the waste by many caravans,
And not, as oft, a lynx-path in a wood
Chance-found, scarce known when found,—a thorn pressed
Against the acacia stem, a palm leaf torn
To its brown wrist, and herbage smoothed one way,
To tell, here passed he, here plunged hard his foot,
Here by the opening crouched for his fell spring
Upon the roe. But as for you, oracle,
Or sign guides your tame feet far from suspense.
For here is one who says : " This is truth's way :
This and no other " : So ye cannot err
Unless ye will. He guides you as a nurse

F

The child, himself within the hourly sound
Of fatherly monition.   But to me,
God cometh as the lightning flashes—now
The arch of heaven shows to its utmost rib,
And now, a void of darkness where I grope,
And kindle my own lights perforce, that flare
And flicker in the wind of circumstance.
Such light was mine, when as I sought to form
A bond betwixt you and the Moabites,
Proving to them a saviour, and to you
A friend, supplying what you lacked of art,
Or skill or beauty in the mode of things.
A double benefit would hence accrue :—
They share your secure shield, ample for both ;
Ye their variety, and so gain force
And manifoldness for your life.   Thereto,
I dreamt of re-uniting ancient kin :—
For are they not indeed your blood ?   And have
Ye always held thus holily aloof ?
Did'st thou not, Moses, in thy trouble seek
The screen of Midianitish tents ?—may hence
Did'st take thy wife, in ripeness of thy will
And unrebuked, from her mild father's care ?
And if some craft were used preparative—
I argue here as one may fairly urge,
Not being of your tribes—ye do not blame
The weaker beasts that use a foil against
Leviathan.   I say there were defects :
Yet need ye deem the whole scope sinister ?
For who can weave a wide and general plan

Of bright threads only ?   Or excluding all
That, judged apart from the contexture, seems
A blot, engage success ?   Doth God himself
Employ no means that, severally viewed,
Touch to the quick our honest sense of wrong ?
Nor need ye think that every coarse extreme
Was proper to the plan, that rather sprang
A bastard-birth of chance, while yet the bloom
Of novelty invited, soon to be
Brushed off, and harmless then.   Yea, I thought,
The initial undue heat will soon die down
Into composed and fair alliances ;
And these twin nations, blended in their fate,
Mayhap, shall countervail decrees of heaven :
Unless, as some fierce thunder-bolt that hastes
Unmoved amid the weeping stars to strike,
His unrelenting will cleaves all the world
To reach its only end :—which I think not.
Yet did I stand prepared at once to own
Arrest of Grace.   If He gives light, I said,
Self-certified as true—or if I now
Am cunningly hoodwinked by policy,
Why certainly Himself will come to me,
And tear the bandage from my eyes ;
Or give a sign to save me, if to shame,
As formerly He did prevent my course
By prodigy.   He will oppose me now—
Raise up a mountain—bid a wide chasm yawn—
Or by great show of power imperative
Dissuade me quite.   For so would I have done,

Had I been God.   Do ye not say He made
A valley in the mighty sea, and cleft
The waters to the primal rock and sand,
For these your Hebrew feet ?   And if my way
Were not His way—nor need I say it—yet
Having conferred with me, as ye have learnt,
Why in my darkness was I left to tread,
Fool-wise, the cliffs' most cruel precipice,
And so slip over life's last foothold thus ?—"
So paused awhile with tightened lips, and eyes
Down-dropt: then with a voice, that sadly fell
On lowest ranges, said " I ask not life :
Your fateful eyes forbid : but answer me—
Thou, Moses, tell me of *His* plan and rule,
If thou wouldst judge me, prophet, righteously."

III.

BALAAM BEFORE MOSES.

THE JUDGMENT OF MOSES.

While Balaam thus his sinuous argument
Warily held, the white-robed conclave sat
Mutely indignant, with eyes hungrily
Half shut, as the ounce-cat's before the prey,
Alert to rise and stone him ere the end
Had the least word or gesture of disdain
Escaped their leader; but as statue high
Of some Egyptian demi-god for ever calm
By temple door, aloof yet present, looks
Superior on all the noisy ways
Of men, so he.   Then with slow words he spake,
The thought preceding in his face as spreads
The lightning-flare abroad before the roll
Of laggard thunder, when the storm is far.
" Our ears have waited on thee, Balaam, fain
To hear what scarce alas! they heard, and learn,
Examining each doubtful syllable,
Thy soul's adhesion to the truth at last.
And once or twice we thought, ' now will he show
How he elects to stand on that sure ground
Where God may find him presently, and bid

Him peace.' But thou hast baffled our desires.—
We have not seen, we trust, thy very heart.
If thou in thoughts retired hast worshipped truth,
Rendering alone thy rites particular,
It may be thou shalt stand acquit to God—
Though how we know not—who thy face may see
Turned in the darkness toward himself.   And this
We hope : yet must we judge thee now perforce
By common clues of speech and act :—thy deeds
We know, and all the world doth know ; thy words
Have heard that seem to us but sinister.

Thou askest of His way, as if His law
Must cease till thou art satisfied that all
In heaven and earth is congruously done ;
And He must let thee hear the morning stars
At song, and show thee all his harmonies ;
Or hold thee free to sound thy part alone—
Discordant if it better pleaseth thee.
But lo He goeth forth in utter light,
Or dwelleth in pavilions high, withdrawn
Where thought may not adventure well, or hides
In twilight kingdoms of the truth unborn,
Inscrutable till time or after-time
Consent ; or in the Vale of Sheol walks
Where all the nodding shadows own Him Lord
Thou hast no eyes to scan His height or depth,
And yet thou hast presumed to dream thy wit
Could bring the Everlasting One within
A compass, and the mighty One constrain,

Drive Him to terms, and by vile strategy
Could subject Him to thy alternatives !
To these who sit around me here to-day,
Lest word of thine should gender doubt, I speak.
In long past years I wedded Zipporah
And took her home with garlands of white broom
And blood-red flowers commingled as of the heart,
Virgin yet warm.   That this pure pact thou wouldst
Besmirch with thy unseemly parallels
I will not stay to urge ; but this I say,
Our tribes are from no later Eden barred
Where grow the fair the living trees of joy.
For know that in the full grown nation's life
Some bane will oft be manifest unseen
In the young race—nay time and circumstance—
Or wicked hands in the dark night may graft
Some poison-yielding wilding of the wood
Upon the trees that God himself did plant.
That Midian serviceable to thy ends,
And in such wise, was found shows well, ingraft
Or native, baseness in the blood, that must
Be purged ere we can welcome them as kin,
Or inter-wed with honour and with peace.

But all was not foreseen, thou sayest.   Ah
Careless was't thou whatever might ensue !
Thou wished'st to be wise as God, but not
As good.   No question that thou knowest well :
Thou knowest, but I fear thou lovest not.
How didst thou venture to degrade thy God

And yet to dream that He would still be God ?
Did meteor flash reveal thee Belial ?
Or following that lynx-path of the truth,
As thou hast said, didst thou find there his dark
Malignant altar reared, and unawares
Pay sacrifice ? Nay, son of Beor. Nay !
Ah by what steps of serpent casuistry
Didst thou from station with the Just and Pure
Descend, contentedly self-blindfolded,
To grovel in a pit of slime ! Behold
God made thee as a king doth make a vase,
All lovely form and hue, for wine of price,
Then breaks the mould and leaves a paragon.
Marred is the only cup and spilt the wine !

And now remains to me a heavy task.
I prophet to prophet speak, yet would not.
Burdens for many weary years I bear,
Wrestling in vain to lift into the light
And fashion for His never-fading crown
The people of His choice, this Israël.
And easier were it for me now to die,
My life for thine a ransom, and so pass
From yoke and furrow to large liberty,
If that He willed. Yet what avail to thee
Would respite prove if still thou wouldst essay
To cast thy threads about, and weave a web
Even for the Lord thy God ? Better the end
Without the hazard. And for this people
Better the end, than thou shouldst stand unscathed

A lawless counsellor against His throne,
A Lucifer unshaken from his seat !
Thee therefore to the sword of righteousness
Before the sun go down I now adjudge,
If these assent.   And still I say ' Let Death
Be Life to thee.' "

           Then at the word of doom,
From mouth to mouth and eye to eye there burst
Fierce gratulation.   But Moses drew his robe
Athwart his face, and they perceived he wept.

A SIXTEENTH CENTURY SHOWMAN.

PREFATORY NOTE.

I must ask my readers to believe that the anachronisms so evident in these two plays are intentional. They are such as abound in the Miracle Plays, upon the pattern of which these are framed.

The same remark applies to the departures from and additions to the sacred narrative.

I may further point out that in compositions of this kind Satan not only constantly figures as the "Villain of the piece," but frequently as the Clown also.

A SIXTEENTH CENTURY SHOWMAN.

A MYSTERY OR MIRACLE PLAY OF THE DEATH OF JOHN THE BAPTIST.

(Speaks in a shrill voice).

Lordyngs, knights, and gentles all,
Squire and reeve, and seneschal,
Ladies fair, and merchants grave,
Come and see these puppets brave :
Though a man be learnèd clerk

I not fear to bid him mark :
Yeomen, craftsmen, if it please ye,
Ye shall find here that will ease ye :
Shepherds wise in any weather,
Lads and lasses come together :
With your golden purses come,
Gather while I beat my drum,
And the piteous story list,
Of the holy John Baptist,
Which these puppets shall declare
Movingly—a picture rare
Of the noble tale of woe.
As the Holy Book doth show :—
Then they shall at my command
Dance for ye a saraband.
Fashioned were they with great skill
In the famousest Seville
By outlandish heathen men
To escape from mickle pain.
For the holy Church had said :—
" Sacrilegious lives ye led !
Now your skill be consecrate
To the Church's good estate !
Semblances of God and Saint,
And of such whose lives attaint
Yield a moral history,
Or a text for homily,
Ye with subtilty shall make,
And escape the bitter stake :
For the Church her wrath restraining

Shall deliver you from brenning."
Ho ! good people all and some
Gather while I beat my drum.
(*Drum beats, and the crowd gathers at the booth*).

SCENE I.

(*Herod and John on the front of the platform. Herodias veiled, and Salome behind. A large green snake presently coils round the group*).

(*Speaks in a natural voice*).

Gentles, we will first present
To your marvellous content
Figures four upon the scene,
Whom the story is between.
Proud Herod in scarlet gown
As a peacock up and down
Stalketh, talketh high and low—
Which way doth the fair wind blow ?
Fore him standeth, meek, yet stout,
Holy John in sheepskin clout.
Famous eremite was he
In the realm of Galilee.
Lo ! he hath no fear to chide
This same king of sinful pride :—
" Thee thy brother's wife to win
Wit ye well is grievous sin."

But ye mark that near the door
Whispering stand two figures more :
One is dark Herodias—

Lo ! there come at Martinmas
Bitter sloes upon the thorn,
Where the pranksome flowers were born—
Scarves of white were her girlánd
Bitter fruit she holds in hand !
She is veilëd for the cause
Scarce we see her as she was.
From her fairness this annoy,
As from Helen's in old Troy.

This her daughter with long hair
Yellow, yellow—swains beware !
When the cheeks are like warm roses,
And the breath is thousand posies,
And the parted lips come home
Kiss ye sweet as honeycomb,
Corydon bethink thee then,
And this story see again !

Ah ! but wherefore now around,
His flat belly on the ground,
Comes yon serpent boding ill ?
See, he crawleth, windeth, till
Crawling, winding, he doth bring
All the four within his ring !
Ah ! ye know it is the green
Snake of Sathanas, I ween.
Thus his circle wide dispread
Surely draws to issue dread.
From his tyranny and thrall
Jesu, Mary, save us all !

Scene II.

*(The banquet. Herod, lords, &c. Salome dances. Herodias
and the snake by the door).*

Here the king at table set
His birthday to celebrate,
With his lords of high degree,
All the pomp of Galilee,
Drinketh sack and hippocras ;
While the dark Herodias
Peereth through the privy cleft
Of the door upon the left ;
And the snake on her doth gloze,
Blinketh, croucheth at her toes,
As he had the poor thrall been
Of this foul accursèd queen.
Cometh through the open door
Damosel ye saw before,
Clapping tabor with her hand—
Fairest flower of all the land,
Lithe as dappled fawn in spring,
Free as west wind gambolling.
Lo ! no seemly dance was this
Fit for Ebrew maid, I wis !
Half the wantonness she made
Is not meet to be displayed.

(Puppet Dances).

Ye may call it serpent dance.
Sathan's power in her glance,

As she writhes and twines about,
Charms with wicked spells the rout
Of these drunken lordyngs, till
She may bow them to her will,
As one taketh in his hand,
Bendeth round a willow wand.
Ah! a lordyng thus a slave
Is no better than a knave!
Look yon swart and doughty carl
With his great neck-chain of pearl!
He would give each one away
At the bidding of this may!
Plucks his russet beard awry,
As she dancing passes by,
Yonder captain of the sea—
Scarcely knows who he may be—
Trembles as a leaf in wind,
Who hath sailed his ship to Ind!
Silksmooth, swollen abbot there,
Squatted in his ivory chair,
Looketh greedily and long—
Hath forgot his evensong.
Sotted Herod, caught with guile,
Rolls his wine-red eyes awhile,
Hiccoughs forth a royal oath,
Plights to her his troth on troth,
That her guerdon for this mirth
Shall be half the kingdom's worth.
Mother-taught she answered straight:
"Though Sir King the night is late,

Yet ye know 'tis meet to slay
Vermin fox by night or day !
Ye shall see your happy vow
Cheaply quit—shall give me now,
Here a golden dish upon
Head of that same traitor John ?
This I ask and will not rue,
I will see if kings be true."—
Laugheth mother through the door,
As the headsman crosseth o'er :
Hisseth snake a little span,
It is all the laugh he can.

SCENE III.

(*The dungeon.   John asleep.   The snake in a corner.   Spiritual
figure of the Virgin Mary.   The executioner*).

Now ye see the dungeon deep
Where the eremite doth sleep,
As a little three year child
That has never been defiled.
In this corner like a log,
But with teeth like mastiff dog,
Sirs, ye see the snake is lying,
So to frighten when a dying
God's dear ward, if that he may.
But there cometh now this way,
Him to comfort hereupon,
Blessed Mary from her Son.

She, the serpent foul espying,
Takes her kerchief white and tying
Round about his grisly head—
Now he seems a dove instead
To the eremite awaking !
He that sign of mercy taking,
As from sleep he wakes anew,
Loudly singeth Allelu !
Mary shining now doth stand
With a lily in her hand
Saying—angel seems she there---
"Come, sweet John, we will to prayer !"
Kneeleth John as in a trance
With a heavenly countenance :
Cometh headsman with the sword
Trembleth he to speak a word ;
Yet in sooth the image real
Of the Virgin spiritual
Seeth not : too gross his sight
For that spectacle of light.
But the bloody deed he wrought
Ye shall follow in your thought.

(*Curtain falls a moment : then procession across the stage*).

Gentles weep not for the spite
Done to this most noble wight.
Life's a bubble, or a vapour,
Or a shy and trembling taper
Blown about by tempest rude.

G

Darkness comes to bad and good !
See the figures hasten by
As in fearful tragedy !
There the damsel bears the dish
Laden with her gruesome wish ;
And the mother follows after
Claps her hands with horrid laughter ;
While the headsman weeps this fate—
Fruit plucked from the tree of Hate.
Yea but Sathan in the rear
Softly slavering doth appear !—
And what after came to pass
Ye shall see as in a glass.

SCENE IV.

One more hand-breadth of the scroll,
Darkly limned, I will unroll.
Ye shall see a miracle,
Or a fearsome parable,
Of what happeth unto men,
Once they enter Sathan's den.
If he gets them in his clew
They shall find him very Jew !
Lo ! he knoweth how to sting
In the mind of churl or king,
And the balm is hard to find
That shall heal a wounded mind.
Mark then, sirs, the judgment sore
On that caitiff king of yore.

(Enter Herod in terror, with uplifted hands, pursued by the snake).

Stay, false Herod !   Wherefore haste ?
Fear you thus to be embraced
By dear friend ?   Lo ! see him glide !
Nay he will not be denied !

(Enter Herodias similarly pursued).

What ! thou purple paramour
Hast thou come unto this hour ?

(Enter Salome with the dish also pursued).

Minion with the honey hair !
Little sin is mickle care !
Thou art led another dance
Thou erst gave so gay joyance !
See ! the dish she overthrows !
Round the head, ah God, there grows
Glory as of pictured saint !
And ye hear a music faint,
While an angel's milk-white arm
Now puts down to seize from harm,
And to heaven bear away,
So to keep till judgment day
This sad relic.   Then these three,
Doubt ye not, shall fronted be
With this token once again.
God His mercy shield us then !

Curtain falls and story's done !
If I have your favours won,
Presently shall be displayed
Famed Duke Jepthah and his Maid.
But to cheer you while ye tarry
After sad thoughts, yea and marry,
While ye all your purses tithe,
These shall jig a dance so blithe,
Ye shall clean forget all sorrow,
Live to-day and not to-morrow,
Bid old wizened Care to flit,
Jog with Sathan to the pit !
Dance yourselves and cry amain
" Goodman showman come again !"

(*All the puppets dance*).

DUKE JEPTHA AND HIS MAID.

SCENE I.

(First of all a Raven flies across the empty Stage. Afterwards Satan appears Dressed as a Monk).

Now your dance is featly done,
Gentles gather every one,
While the story I unfold,
Of a famous knight of old,
Jeptha hight, and of his deed
That so grisly was and drole,
Ye shall have a thing to tell
To your gossips on the selle,
By and by, when cometh snow,
And the belling wind doth go
Round the closèd house again,
Like a wolf in hunger-pain.
Praise or blame—how should it fall ?
Question passeth as a ball
Tossed by maidens in a ring,
Neath the apple trees in spring,
Till each hand becometh slack
Criss-a-cross returning back.
Ye will joy at this my tale
As at song of nightingale,

While ye see with what device
It is passioned to your eyes,
And will say when it is past,
Best wine, soothly, cometh last.

SCENE I.

Mark ye how yon bird doth bring
O'er the scene a shadowing ?
Men do think him devil-taught,
Wise in evil, if in aught.
But ye keep the honest road,
Lordyngs, and may laugh at bode.
Natheless if he cross your way
Ye will handsel prayer that day.
Hie away presageful fowl !
Enters Sathan in a cowl.
Sathan !   Sathan !   Thou art guessed !
Think not in such habit dressed
To beguile this company.
Fie upon thy villainy !

*(The Cowl is drawn back from the Head of the Puppet that
seems to Speak, the Showman Ventriloquising).*

" Since ye know me, gentles mine,
And this guise so soon divine,
I will shew a thing or two
Of mine art, to pleasure you.
Anciently men told of one
Protis naméd, who could don
Shape on shape, more merrily

Than the waves of the salt sea ;
Or the clouds that build a town
For a moment, then pluck down
All the palaces, then rear
A hill, a mountain, to the sphere,
Which while yet your mind revolves
Into a white bird dissolves,
That with great wing bears away—
While you might an Ave say.
I am Protis : I will change
'Fore your eyes more swift and strange."

(Changes successively into a Serpent, a Fair Woman, a King, an Angel, a Knight-at-Arms).

(As a Serpent). " Such I was when longing Eve
Without apples could not live.

(A fair Woman). Such I was when David saw
From his window Bathsheba.

(A King). Such, when He, I may not name,
Into the wild desert came.

(An Angel). Such I am S. Poule doth say
Often in the light of day.

(A Knight). Such I will be in a trice
At Duke Jeptha's sacrifice."

SCENE II.

(Jeptha and his Warriors returning home, are met by his Daughter, and Maidens following).

Masters see Duke Jeptha come
With his knights unto his home.

He hath sworn an oath to bring
Whatsoever household thing
Issues from his palace door,
When he cometh conqueror,
Though it be of dearest price
It shall be a sacrifice.
Now appeareth singing blithe
As a laverock, when the scythe
Which the early mower wields,
In the red-lit morning fields,
Swishing slowly to and fro,
Lays the scented swaths arow,
Daughter dear—a rose is she,
Only rose upon his tree.
Vermeil tincture on her lip,
Honeydew for love to sip ;
Blue her eye as hyacint,
In dark copses, when the glint
Of the nice and dainty sun
Singles out an only one ;
And above her forehead proud,
Like a burnished morning cloud,
Softly shone her combèd head ;
Whence her locks unfilleted
Flowed unto her kirtle green.
Gracious was her body's mien :
Lithe each limb and sinew true,
As a master bow of yew,
Answers to the archer's hand.
She was at her own command,

In the kingdom of her mind,
For each deed of virtuous kind.
Traitorous thought she held aloof
As misfitting all behoof,—
To herself, her kindred own,
And the High God on His throne.
She was wondrous clean, and yet
Lest ye think of her as set
In the angel's cold degree,
Certes she was womanly.
Yea already on the string
Arrow, feathered with the wing
Of a turtle dove for grace,
Hath Dan Cupid set in place.
See ye not yon ruddy squire ?
Sooth ye mote of him enquire.
But behold how in the rear
Damsels bearing music gear,
Not too closely following,
Te Deum laudamus sing,
Thereto dancing seemëly.

(Pause while the Dance proceeds).

Ye have seen how in the sky
Of midsummer unsuspect,
With no cloud bedimmed or fleckt,
Smooth and clean as lady's glass,
Suddenly it comes to pass
That a storm uplifts its head,
Like a great curse long delayed,

Sucking darkness in its sweep ;
Then before the lightnings leap
On the field and on the town,
Sheds amazing twilight down.
Ah Duke Jeptha what is this ?
Yea the tongue a rudder is
Guiding ship to weal or shame,
As declares th' apostle Jame.
From thine own mouth springeth doom.
Vain thou weepest.   Curse is come !

(Veils of dark blue descend and close the Scene).

SCENE III.

(A   Castle.   Jeptha's Daughter sings at a Window.   The Squire approaches and urges her to fly.   She refuses. The Showman sings her song in a lamentable falsetto).

SONG.

" Bend low your heads ye daffodils,
   In soft gold pastures crowding ;
Ye red-eyed daisies weep anew :—
   To morrow is my shrouding.

Yet wear your blooms for all your day,
   The careless earth adorning :
Though I shall know no eve or noon,
   Since midnight comes at morning."

Lordyngs ye shall hear the sighing
Of these lovers fond replying :
Two things chiefly man desireth
Speech concerning — Love and Death !

He " Haste O haste, undo the wicket,
 Let us fly to yonder thicket ! "

She " Gentle youth, I am no bride.
 Therefore will I here abide."

He " Love, I will thee holy keep,
 Till we may the guerdon reap."

She " Ah, sir squire, I am not free
 To accept your courtesy."

He " Let us flee to th' Amorites,
 They will grant us marriage rites ! "

She " Nay, now nay, ungentle youth !
 I may not be false to truth."

He " O but hearken : Be my wife !
 It is but one step to life ! "

She " Many steps from truth 'twould be,
 If I were to follow thee."

He " O but think what 'tis to die !
 Without life's felicity ! "

She " Death I know not : God I know,
 And I fear me not to go."

He " Think, it is thy father's word !
 Not the doom of heaven's high Lord."

She " Sir, my father's word hath gone
 To the high God on his throne ! "

He "Is it then a just decree?"

She "Ask not my simplicity!"

He "Yet once more, I thee conjure."

She " Nay, my heart is very sure,
But for that, though scarcely spoken,
Each heart gave the other token,
Now ere yet I hence remove,
Sir, I say that you I love!"

(She goes away).

He "Darkness, darkness! Death and Hell!
Ye have covenanted well!"

*(Enter train of Damsels with dishevelled hair and heads
dejected. They more slowly across the Stage)*.

SCENE IV.

*(Jeptha's Daughter bound. An Altar set. Satan in disguise
of a knight kindles the fire. Presently S. George appears)*.

O it is a heavy day!
Welaway and welaway!
Song birds hush, and the sad wind
Tells the tale of fate unkind,
Through the woods and on the hill,
In the field and by the mill,
Whispers low where Juda's halls,
Stand adread of what befalls.
As a jewel of great price

Flashing in the common eyes,
Yet possessëd by some one,
Deeming it a paragon ;
Dear and only, matchless fair
She was to her father there.
Yet stands Jeptha without sound,
Glareth he around, around,
Like a lion in a pit,
Without force to better it.
Masters, see the altar high,
And the faggots on it lie !
Know ye not yon cursëd foe,
Striving at the tinder box ?
　　Dearest, faithful maid prepare,
He ne pity will nor spare !—
Lord how leaps the hungry flame !—
Hold you there, in God his name !
Look, who cometh ?　Bright his sword
With the anger of the Lord !—

(*St. George appears, drives Satan away, scatters the fire, and
dismantles the Altar*).

"Weke-weke" ! Sathan, dost thou cry ?
Shrewd the stroke that made thee fly !
Fly back to the burning lake,
Let thy dam assuage thy ache !
　　But this noble puissant Saint
　　Would now utter his intent.

　　　S. George loq.
"Jeptha, and ye men of war,

I have this day journeyed far
To relieve a worthy maid
From the ban upon her laid.
Devil's cunning hath been foiled :
Jeptha, thou art now assoiled :
Maiden, thou art free to wed :

(*The Squire unbinds the Maid and leads her aside*).

God his mercy is displayed !
But ye see how man may set
For his feet a dreadful net,
That shall tangle him in wrong
Through the mischief of the tongue.
Whence, Sir Duke, to holy church,
That ye may be free from smirch
In the eyes of men, and seal
All your inward penitence
By some action clear to sense,
Ye shall give, by my command,
Forty rood of pasture land.
As this season, year by year,
Back returns, ye shall appear
Sackcloth girded, holding Psalter,
Fore the sacrificial altar ;
And, while all men do admire,
Tongue of beast into the fire,
Emblem of thy folly past,
With thine own hands thou shalt cast."

(*All the Figures bow as the Scene closes*).

Epilogue.

Ere I take my leave of ye,
Gentles, show your courtesy !
Largess, lordyngs !—Noble sir
Thanks to you !—And you mastér !
Thanks to each one !   When I next
Work my puppets to a text,
And these trappings gay unfurl,
It shall be unto an Earl.
If he wink or wave his hand,
He a thousand can command.
(Still I hear the money clink.
Thanks again !) so ye may think,
Ye have been in next degree,
Unto famous company.
While your favours still prevail,
I will tell a wee-bit tale.
Once me asked a greybeard man :—
" Read my riddle, if you can.
Lo ! I do a dragon keep
Within fence, by wake or sleep.
The old wife hath one to fit ;
But she hath no fence for it.
So the beast doth scramble out,
And doth give me many a bout."
"Sir," quoth I, " what mote it be ? "
Then he oped his mouth to me,
Showed his foul tongue to the root,
And the villain teeth to boot.
Ah ! he was a scurril knave.—
Thanks, my masters, God you save.

SOLOMON SENESCENS.

Here on this throne unparalleled of power,
Renown and wisdom, happily conjoint,
Watching myself and all the world grow old,
I sit, revolving many things that were and are :
Yet in the multitude of thoughts that rise
I scarce do sorrow that I sorrow not
To have declined a little from the height,
Whither I soared at early morn : so rich
Hath life's experience been.   Yea though a voice
Persists it had been wisdom to forego
Life's amplitude, so reach the highest height ;
And I must needs assent : yet stands my choice.
God must forgive me that I sorrow not.
I marvel truly that with me of late
A certain dryness at the heart forbids.
Perhaps the fount is sealed awhile, and will
Break forth in gracious feeling presently.
But thought and sight are chiefest, I opine.

Let me remember how I stood and stand
In the same lot of grace God gave at first,
Through all the years growing from more to more,
In name and fame and glory visible.
For let me hold, as I may verily,
That there hath been some counterpart within

Of all the state magnifical, and praise
Orbed by the voices of the world. What if
The tally be not close, seeing the mind
Of man is vain ? Should I sit here if God
Did not approve ? This throne expresses His !
I will believe that all is well ; though, like
Heart-searching tremors through a sleeping house
When quakes the earth, terror hath shaken me
In hours of peace, as I had never found
Footing of truth. And, specially, it wrought
When first the Temple like a lily bloomed,
Each golden petal answering the sun ;
And I, as Daysman of the Kingdom set,
Offered the flower to God, with sacrifice
And prayer, typing, as all men thought, a new
Melchizedek. For ere the concourse thawed
There pressed before me one who craved to speak,
Posing as prophet, and forthwith, " O King,"
He said, " I saw of late a miracle,
Which God hath bid me show to Solomon :
For thou art wise, and skilled to read all signs,
As Joseph thy so great forefather was.
It happened then, O king, but yester noon,
When looking from my chamber in the east,
I saw an eagle circling in mid-air,
That narrowing the wheel of his broad vans
Approached the earth, until at length he took
The edge of a dry water-pit : therein
Was hid a little space while one might say
With praise the holy decalogue. And thence

H

Arising flew with mighty waft of wing
Against the sun, and vanished in the light
A moment; then came falling from the heavens
With direful curves, and half-retrievals vain,
Until, plumb as a stone, he dropt to earth.
Then I ran forth to see this sight, and lo !
From underneath the bird there crawled a snake.
So I took knowledge of the thing, that when
In evil hour the bird had sought the pit
The cruel worm had writhed upon his claws,
And, carried thence far in the sky, had stung
Him at the heart.   But what the wisdom is
I say not : 'Tis for thee, O king.'   So ceased,
And, while we pondered, presently was gone ;
But there remained I know not what of fear,
That back returned for many days ; nay till
The years had passed, and proved the omen false.
For still I reign with glory undecayed.
But if his parable were rather meant
A fateful forecast of life's better life—
Yet hath the sequel followed ?   I confess
Some declination ; for to retrograde
From what we worship best in our green youth,
And fondly hope, is but the way of life.
So, if the heart hath lost some force, again,
It is the wearing of the hour.   My soul
Doth crave no more, fretting in its small house,
To compass royally, and wed somewise,
All precious things unto herself.   Content
She marvels always, as with large clear eye

She sees the sparkling universe.   For time,
Destroying, not destroys the sight, the thought,
The estimate that links with God who made.
Still I behold the fairness everywhere,
Various, opposite, indifferent
Thus far, that each particular so rounds
The total view, as not to be excised.
I mark the joy of softly-hollowed sky,
Of hills where angels tread, and fields
That hold the sun, the private gesture of each plant,
The visages distinct of bird and beast;
Nor shrink I from the dragon-haunted sea
And coiling deep, the war of adverse clouds,
Nor whatsoever dark tremendous thing
Supplies the contrary of fairest fair.
Still I appraise—still catch the subtle sense
Of Lilith's twitching robe, her glance oblique,
And gleam evasive of the ivory flesh,
So questioningly, questionably coy :
The grace I see : the blood no longer stirs :
Though much I marvel at the wisdom dark
Of beauty diverse from the best.   Perfect
I saw but once.—Ah ! Shulomith if thou
Hadst left thy vintage toil and rustic troth
For me to drop the honey in thy mouth,
Perfect I had not seen.—But all the way
Of man I mark.   It is no sin to see
The good of all—to see it and to say.
I find not falsehood absolute but mixed
With precious grains of truth.   Nay oft the art

Of man surrounds some mystery of God
With make-believe of falsehood, lest too soon,
Too widely, should the truth be known, and lose
The rarity and preciousness at once,
And thus in alien rites there may be seen
Divine inclosures, hidden long ago ;
And whoso finds them doubly finds, because
Of contrast and surprise : as when men bring
From Lebanon those rugged spheres and gorms—
You break them, and behold within, ablaze,
Are beryl, topaz, hyacinthine stars,
Threads of the rainbow, fingers of the sun
And moon : You find them, and delight doth make
Them doubly yours. So have I broke the shell
Of these mis-shaped idolatries to learn
Thoughts of the wise, concealed from ancient time,
And note with marvel God in many forms.

So then the son of Nebat flees betimes
To his Egyptian eyrie ! I had thought
To cage the pert young osprey, and clip wing,
And claw ! Now will he nurture his resolves,
Until full grown in craft and naughtiness,
Spreading his insolent wing once more,
He will return to vex the land : nor he
Alone : but not in my day, as I think.
We see the long-projected shadow cast
Of storm to come, while we sit in the sun.
Verily 'twere not wise to trammel up
The future with the hour of present peace.

My son must heed.   Meanwhile our throne remains :
No fall is here for tale or chronicle,
Or parable, with sigh and halting breath !
No death in life, though slowly fades the flush
That crimsoned youth—abatement natural !
And therefore all is well, no doubt, despite
The surly prophet and his apologue.

Ho ! Ethan ! tell the Persian sage to seek
The ivory summer house at eve, and let
Him bring the astrolabe—but secretly.
His art is curious, though perhaps he lies.

THE WEDDING GARMENT.

Not a cloud or vapour dim
From the zenith to earth's rim !
Smooth the heaven's countenance
Like to prophet's in a trance !
Or to vestal's in her calm,
When she saith the prayer or psalm,
And with heaven in her eye
Droopeth into ecstasy !
Hangs the moon's fair coronet
In the skies mid-violet !
Never beamed so rich an argent,
To young lovers by the margent
Of the dear enchanted shore ;
Never on the russet moor
Waking shepherd with delight
Bathed in such a fountain bright !
As from all the world's wide ways,
Stained with travel, length of days,
Came they, when the night was late,
To the great King's palace gate.
High above them glisten walls,
Shafts, and columns, pedestals,
Mighty towers, and spires at last,

Till the sense of sight is past,
Irised with the hues that deck
In the spring the wild dove's neck ;
But with silver shimmering
Of the moonlight's burnishing.
Yet the light was still more fair
Where it met the torches' flare
In the many lattices—
Turned them all to topazes.
Now the gate swings wide to all
On its hinges musical ;
And they go unto the feast
From the greatest to the least ;
While the minstrels in their order
Breathe upon the low recorder,
On the drum make joyful stir,
Stroke the silver dulcimer,
Gaily harp and zither twang,
Bells and cymbals loudly clang
As they march the guests before
Through each sounding corridor.
Now they thrid a muffled aisle
Where the music halts awhile,
In the darkness quivering,
As the shadow of a wing
Cast by bird beneath the sun,
When he fills the highest throne.
Till, emerging from the gloom,
Enter all the presence-room,
Where the light is more than day,

Here they stand in meek array,
Whilst is heard the room around
Silver simmer of sweet sound :
Viols plead with tender cry,
Harp and lute expectant sigh,
Murmur anxiously the drums—
Strains prelusive till he comes.

Mighty was that King, yet mild,
Truth, and honour undefiled,
Justice firm, and wisdom clear,
In his face sublime appear—
Royal will and empery
Blended with benignity.
Slow he treads the populous hall —
' O, my friends, I welcome all
To this high solemnity,
Who have come in charity ;
But from this our feast to-day
Must one spot be purged away,'—
Pausing then in awful sadness.
Each one doubting his own gladness,
Questions, as he passes by,
Tremulously, ' Is it I ?'
But the intruder, speechless held,
By his contrast stands revealed,
In his sordid raiment dight,
All the rest in caftans white —
As a raven from the rock
Mid a pigeons' milky flock.

Then the King, his speech resuming—
'In what pride, on what presuming,
Friend without the garment meet,
Hast thou come unto my seat?'
Silence then, and beating hearts,
Whilst the guest in shame departs,
From the feast, the song, the light,
Into solitary night.——
Now the moon is in her grave;
Cloud on cloud, and wave on wave,
Knits the tempest, warp and woof,
Cerements for the starry roof.
From the lonely fields arise
Wind-borne, wind-torn elegies,
Spirit-breathed—'O, had I known'—
(While the wind's sad undertone
Swells and falls, but does not cease)—
'What belonged unto my peace'—
(Then, as with a world of sighs)—
'Hid for ever from mine eyes!'

LEGEND OF S. CHRISTOPHER.

The old legend of St. Christopher appears, as might be expected, in various forms. The version I follow is briefly this :—Offerus, a heathen, and a man of immense stature, resolved to devote his strength to the greatest of kings. In pursuance of this purpose he entered the service of the Emperor of Christendom. But presently, finding that the Emperor was afraid of the devil, Offerus entered the service of the latter, as being greater than the Emperor. And they twain, the legend says, went round the world, until, coming to a spot where the Cross was erected, he discovered that the devil trembled at that sign. Therefore Offerus determined to embrace the service of Christ as greater than all. Ignorant, but ardent, he wandered in the quest of his new master; but ultimately gave himself to works of charity, as will be told. Nor was his wish to see Christ granted, save as also the story will say.

———

I.

S. CHRISTOPHER AT THE FORD.

I, Offerus, once heathen, now of Christ,
Still wait for Him. At first I said, 'Declare

But where he lives, and I will scale all hills,
And cross all seas, to come unto His seat
—Aye, though a thousand monsters bar the way.'
(In the fierce pride of youth, I doubted not
To deal with all, as with the lions twain
That loomed against me on the Libyan sand,
Whilst a scant moon just showed their burning eyes ;
When by the mane the lordly male I seized,
And swung him, hammerwise, against his mate
—Dashed both to silence and to vulture meat.)
    For many held that Christ had come again ;
And whispers ran about the dark world then,
As sparks that quicken on a half-quenched brand,
Of a strange budding forth of grace divine,
With radiant blooms of special miracle.
So when men said, 'Lo ! here is Christ or there,'
I journeyed, on the mere report, to find
The substance of the tale attenuate—
Resolved into the glamour of dim woods,
Where myriad pine stems cozen still the eye
Or glimmer of marsh lights, or shadow seen
By caves and hollows of the moonlit hills,
Or, at the best, a vision in a dream.
Thereto, the portents manifold forsook
Their bulk and hue, and fell into the list
Of daily things.   Thus sought I, bearing cold
Beyond dim Thulë, at the end of things,
Where the untravelled snows retain
The flushing of the indignant sunless skies ;
Or, wand'ring farther than the swallow flits,

Gaining at length some orient land of fire,
Gasped for the shadow of great rocks in vain.

    And yet my soul gasped more for Christ, nor ceased
The hunger and the thirst to see His face,
Before His feet to fall, nor ceased the quest
By weary land and sea, until the wheel
Of Time brought round the Autumn of my age.
For wisdom, as the crude fruit of the sloe
That ripens not before the frosts begin,
Delayed with me : until I chanced on one
Who said, 'Thy Lord would rather thou shouldst do
The least thing in His house below, than run
For ever to the door to see Him come.'

    Wherefore I only wait ; nor curdle life
With vehement desire, returning void.
But by this riverside abide in peace,
And carry pilgrims, shoulder-borne, across
The flood, for love's sake, and until He comes.

S. CHRISTOPHER AND THE CHILD.

Bent somewhat from the straight of youth, with arms
Scarce equal to the tasks of former years,
When he would take a fifth year sapling oak
And twist it snakewise to the earth, yet stood
The old man by his door, like Greek god carved
For temple frieze, that puts to glorious shame
Some sculptor's shed, ere it be placed. All day,
As with loud horns and trumpets pealed the wind ;
Arrowlike fell the rain. He looked across
The tawny water by the ford, where die
Day's lights the last, and marked the solid stream
As if some lake among the hills, wide, deep,
Through conduit cut by sudden earthquake thrust,
Bodily slipped by. The young moon's frail skiff,
That in her going forth with free prow sailed,
Now foundered in the black sea overhead.
O then with open diapason wind,
And stream victoriously shouted ! He,
Withdrawing soon, enkindled his small lamp
And sat to read : the parchment, his one prize,
Yellow with age's amber, spread : intent,
With large slow finger, traced each mystic word :

'Descended rain, blew wind, rushed floods, and beat
Upon that house, that fell not, founded on
A rock.' 'Thou art my Rock,' he said, 'O Christ!'
Loud roared the tempest round that cabin rude ;
But in the wake of that vast sound a cry,
Feeble and piteous, of lost child, or lamb.
Rising, he girt his loins, and touched the latch.
Again, distressful, pleading, sobbing came,
In the wind's pauses, that shrill call.   He grasped
His staff, and hastened forth into the night.

Next morning pilgrims coming to his door,
Not open as was wont, entered and saw
The strong man drawing to his end.   To these
He, with a humble, yet exalted air,
Declared what had befallen.   Even this :
That crossing the wild river he had found
A tender boy, who wept and did not speak ;
Whom taking on his shoulder scarce he held
Above the tossing water of the ford,
For little compass had the infant's arms,
And deeper ran the river than before,
And fiercer blew the wind across the pines.
While as he fought the flood, intolerable
The burden of the child became, until
His neck was bowed unto the leaping surge.
But when he thought to cast away the child—
It was a shame he might not do.   Therefore
He called on God.   So gained, sore spent, the shore.

When lo ! a wonder was revealed to him—
Panting he slid the little one adown
—Straightway, serene, august, indued with light,
Glorious in mould, the child transfigured stood,
Who said with sweetness, 'Inasmuch as thou,
O man, wouldst do this thing for My least child
Know then thou hast performed it unto Me.
Not Offerus, but Christopher, shall men
Call him, who bore the Christ across the flood.'

III.

S. CHRISTOPHER'S DEPARTURE.

I, Christopher, speak now to you, my friends,
Tremblingly my new name.   Perhaps this crown
Had been too bright to wear, had life remained ;
But now I go at once before the throne,
Nor stay to lose the wonder of the grace.
      Returns to-night, how clearly o'er the years,
The misty April wood, asteam with scent
Of opening leaves, and a blue world of flowers,
Where the grave palmer found me in the sun,
Wearied with hunting in the earlier morn—
I, in my thought and wish scarce more than flesh ;
And he, God's swordsman keenly to divide
The flesh and spirit, with a word.   For he,
Observing me, like a felled oak (he said),
Cried, ' Noble were this strength, if nobly used,
For Christ and Truth.'   Whereat I rose abashed,
Pricked somewhere in the sluggish soul of me ;
While yet rejoicing that he praised my strength,
Discerning dimly greater end of life
Might be, than hunting of the stag and boar
—More lasting fruit of this one gift of mine.
I echoed, ' Christ and Truth': strange names, new powers,
That urged me forth to seek, I scarce knew what.

For yet he added, seeing me a child
In knowledge and in art, 'Take thou a yoke
Upon thy wildness, and learn thou to serve.'
While I—'The greatest will I serve, none less.'
He smiled and went his way to some far shrine.
Dubiously exploring my new path,
I came to Rome.—And Rome returns to-night!
—The flickering wraith of the pale king—the groups
Of masks surmounting robes pontifical,
Or knightly harness, by the throne.   Bad days
Were those, when goodness seemed a caitiff thing
—Evil imperially glittered, night
And day, a presence with me to control !
When I, not able to endure the mixed
Lights of the time, ran back into the dark !
(Merciful God, Thou hast passed by those days !)
    Returns the way-side cross, whereby I sat
Invoking Him until the evil presence fled,
Return the many lands, the far-off isles,
I sought, till that I reached this spot of peace.
    Yet now I know I must fare forth again—
But ye, my friends, are ye not multiplied ?
Do ye not wear your festal robes to-day ?
The cabin fills !—O friends I greet you all !—
Now make ye way, and follow to the stream—
Ah God, a deeper stream ! *But He bears me !*

"I WILL SUP WITH HIM AND HE WITH ME."

Fell the night on field and river:
Scarce one trembling star did quiver,
'Twixt the closing lids of day,
On the traveller's darkling way;
When I saw a form approaching,
Through the wild-wood fast encroaching
On my garden's proper bound,
Where no fruit, alas! was found.
Oh, the garden of my sowing!
Roots of bitterness were growing,
Leafage for a fading crown;
But no plant of true renown.
Then the summons came, expected
By my heart's fear, and rejected
Ere I heard him call my name,
In those tones that shook my frame
—Blended tones of trumpet pealing
Battlewise; then, gently stealing,
Pleading after clangour sharp,
Tones as of a human harp.
Thus I answered, respite gaining,
To my old thought troth maintaining,
"Hence! Away! the night is late!
Quit these precincts desolate!

Quenched upon my hearth each ember,
Here for thee is no guest chamber :
Bread unleavened, and for wine
Water of affliction, mine !"
Churlish, evil was my greeting;
But methought I heard the beating
Of a kind heart through the door,
As he called my name once more.
"From a far land have I sought thee,
And in pity have I brought thee
Living water, living bread
Such as ne'er thy fathers fed."
Then the door I opened slowly,
And the Unknown meek and lowly,
Sprinkled o'er with soft starlight,
Entered from the purple night.
Light came with him, light prevailing
More and more, as when unveiling,
Breaking through the cloudy fleece,
Shines the moon with vast increase.
Then, O heart, to thy surprising,
Vanished all thy ill surmising,
As amidst that tranquil light
Stood disclosed thy Lord to sight ;
And, when uttered the Hosanna,
Thy bread broken seemed as manna : —
And thou drankest draughts of peace
From the founts that do not cease.
"Kinsman," said He, "younger brother,
No Redeemer hast thou other,

From thy sorrow and thy sin,
Than whom scarce thou tookest in.
But if I, thy poor life sharing,
Through this first world with thee faring,
Hallow thus thy daily life,
Give thus peace instead of strife,
Thou with me, beyond dim Hades,
Past the dread vale where death's shade is,
Through the long long days of heaven,
Shining each with light of seven,
Shalt sit down, with spirits vestal,
By joy-rivers clear as crystal—
'Neath the spreading boughs of bliss
Pluck the golden fruit, I wis,
Where the Tree of Life doth stand,
Sing the New song in that land."

CÆDMON.

I.

A herdsman was I—russet prophet now,
As by the rede of Holy Writ was he,
Who cropped the meagre fruit of sycamores,
Amos, God's spokesman in the ancient days,—
A forthright soul, who, not with sword and bow,
But with great strokes of words dealt mightily ;
So I unskilful sing on these harsh shores,
And God doth round my rude song to His praise.
    Prophet in some sort : though I may not say
    God singeth thus by me ; yet sing I thus
    By God. This tongue by Him is marvellous :
    These eyes and ears are urged to sharper sense
    By the great over-Lord, as day by day,
    Thrall-like they wait in His Divine Presénce.

II.

Shamefaced among my fellows at the feast,
I sat as fool, the proper scorn of all.
" Come twang thy harp," they cried, " thou silent guest :
Strike but one spark from that dull soul of thine."
I fled the hall, and said " Yea beast to beast !"
And slept among the oxen of the stall.

That self-same night a vision came and blest
With new aspéct my spirit saturnine.

    "Cœdmon arise," one said, "and sing thy hymn.
To me the tongue e'en of the dumb shalt sing."
"Alas," I said, "I have no song to bring!"
"Nay thou shalt sing," said he, "the order slow
Of the world's story, to its ending dim."
I woke God's minstrel in the world below.

BEZALEEL.

Oft have I walked o' nights around the camp—
The folded flock of Hebrew tents—alone,
To mark where, heart-like, in the midst there stood,
Glowing beneath a fiery-tinted cloud,
The dwelling of Jehovah, pausing then
To muse how mine own works were there enshrined,
Yet hidden always from mine eyes—the lamp
Of gold with branches seven, like a fair tree,
With bowls made like unto the almond flowers
Dimpled by God's own hand; and the great veil
With banded colours of the sky and clouds,
Disclosing figures of the cherubim
To represent the wisdom manifold,
And worship of the world—all wrought by me,
And by Aholiab of Dan.   But chief
Have I recalled the wistful forms of gold,
With outstretched wings above the ark, that bow
For ever in the darkness of the shrine,
Even as my spirit bows before the Lord.
Thus stirred, have I lived o'er again the time
When God's power mastered us, yet left us free
(Not men the less, because so full of God)
So that in line and curve, clustered or sole,
From angel faces to the ruby seeds
Of split pomegranates, all the forms were wrought

In truth, with uttermost of patient grace.
(It is the last fine touch that makes divine)
While in the wholeness of the measured parts
And correspondences, the final work
Contained a parable, that all the wise
Might read of the great building of the world.
Then as a sharp sword piercing comes the thought
" Yea, this has been thy history :—Upborne
A brief while to the gates of heaven and day !
Then falling wingless to the twilight world !
The joyous forms of god-like thoughts have passed !
Thy fruits and flowers are but earth's common yield,
Without a hint of Paradise to-day !" ·
Yet have I had my past !   God moved through me !
The barren days succeeding have no power
To blot the richness of the scroll's first line.
But in the dreams and visions of the night
Some messenger of grace has seemed to say
(The Lord forgive if that his servant errs)
"Thou and Aholiab were set for signs,
Beyond the purpose of those works ye did,
Of days not yet revealed, when not alone
The elders of your tribes, and priests within
The verge of sanctities ye see not ; but,
Weavers, artificers, and craftsmen all,
Yea, and the common men that tend the sheep
And bear the burdens of a menial life,
Shall be anointed for their various work,
And live under the very breath of God
In those great days that lie beyond your ken."

A LONDON ARTISAN.

In Tenebris.

I "OUGHTN'T?" Why oughtn't? I tell you it's bred in
  the bone!
Blame my "inherited impulses," doctor! leave *me* alone,
For I know what passions from birth, and before that,
  wrought in my dust—
The fire, that drink cannot quench, the worm never dying
  of lust.
My father, men say, was a devil, who loved to sully the
  white
Of souls that believing gave all, as they thought, to an
  angel of light:
And my mother, poor soul, was a weakling who madly
  struggled to save
Some rags and tatters of virtue, then drank herself into
  her grave.

Not many minutes to live, do you say? All right! Let
  us finish up well!
I'll give you a toast—gin or brandy?—the abolition of
  Hell!
Though I would there were something in store for the
  man who gave me this life,
And murdered the body and soul of her he should have
  made wife.

Aye but I felt rather queer when the parson was telling
　his tale !

Fancies I had that made my cheek turn, like enough, a bit
　pale !

For he talked about sin, as if 'twere an actual living
　thing :—

A serpent he called it that stings souls like fate, and will
　sting !

And I felt the beast coiled round my heart-strings, roll
　upon roll,

Throttling me, poisoning me—aye the very blood of my
　soul.

Then he talked about Him too, doctor, you know whom I
　mean,

Till I saw his face plain as daylight, and cursed my folly
　and sin—

Such a face !—so sad-like, and I thought he was sorry for
　me,

And it near broke my heart to think what I had been—
　might be.

So I swore if he'd help me and save me out of my fears

I'd turn a new leaf that night, and blot it only with tears.

And thinks I—there's Lucy—I'll be a better man to her
　now, poor lass !

And the children—nay Thomas Briggs not ever another
　glass !

And the devil says he to me, " You never mind, old pal !

Don't all the clever men tell you straight there aint no
　hell ?

Have thy fling, man! Its natur', I tell thee, and natur'
    will rule.

Leave religion to women, and don't be a methody fool."

Eight o'clock do you say—morning? It ought to be
    light.—

Doctor, I say, suppose after all the parson was right?—

There's a sound at the door like a great flood roaring and
    tumbling—hark!

Doctor, I say, can you pray?—my God—O it's dark!—

FATE, LAW, AND CHRIST.

"Proserpina plumbea pede."
"Rarò antecedentem scelestum
Deseruit pede Pœna claudo."—HORACE.

"There is no such thing as spontaneousness in nature."—TYNDALL.
"Mercy and truth are met together; righteousness and peace have
kissed each other."—PSALM LXXXV., 10.

I.

They said of old that Fate was sure,
And by no craft of man was balked ;
For though with leaden foot she walked,
She reached at last the sinner's door.
With leaden foot, but iron will,
Where'er the guilty man might dwell,
And fondly hope that all was well,
With faultless scent, she followed still.
He wandered haply o'er the sea,
And bought and sold with large increase,
And clad him in the robes of peace :
—The trail is all confused, thought he,
And gaily carolled—dreamt no wrong :
The uneasy self within his breast
He stroked, and soothed and sang to rest :
"Dear soul, now saunter life along !

"Joy-harvests shall be now thy due !
Nor blasting storms on this new path,
Like winter on the aftermath,
For thy forgotten sin ensue !"
And so, it might be, long years ran
A harmless course, and joined the past :
Then her fierce cry rang out at last,
"Lo ! this the hour, and this the man ?"
Thus said they in the olden time—
And still they sang how Zeus the great,
Above the Fury and the Fate,
Sat ever on his throne sublime ;
Who aye reserved some royal space
(Though lesser gods would oft perplex
With jealousies and counter checks)
Wherein to show a suppliant grace ;
—Pure freedom's uncontrolled domain,
Where Fate-tossed souls might shelter find
And prayer from a submissive mind,
With offerings meet, might answer gain.

II.

A modern page I read of late
—How Law the universe controls ;
The soulless taskmaster of souls,
More terrible than ancient Fate,
Extremer, swifter, stronger far,
To whom mechanic government
All powers and forces yield assent
And ministering agents are.

Yea, Law, I read, is Zeus to-day;
There is no other god than *It*:
The cold *Impersonal* doth sit
And watch the erring world alway.
A thousand tribes their woes rehearse,
Cry to high heaven's remorseless bars,
Cry to the unavailing stars,
Cry through the Arctic universe :
"Is there no Heart that bids us *Come*?
No greater Soul to answer soul ?"
From sphere to sphere, from pole to pole,
The new Divinity is dumb;
Nor smiles, nor grieves for men below;
Knits action and the consequence;
And knows no pulse of difference
As the great æons come and go.
An image in a changeless calm,
It turns not from its awful loom;
But weaves the life of man with doom,
And heeds not breath of prayer or psalm.
—Not more unmoved the silent sphinx
When chants of passing pilgrims rise;
Or when the drowning sailor's cries
Are borne across the sandy links.
The wise men raise their pæans—"Hail!
Thou hear'st us not, eternal Mute!
Yet will we sing the Absolute,
Unknowable, Ironical!
Strange Lord art thou of Helicon!
Strange source of love, at love that mocks!

The Everlasting Paradox !
The Infinite Automaton !"

If this be god essentially,
Alas that I was ever born !
Or "suckled in a creed outworn"
Had not long ages ceased to be !

III.

On lonely hills I wandered forth,
Beneath a low and burdened sky :
In gloomy file swept slowly by
Titanic clouds from out the north,
And settled round the dark concave :
Between, the thunder-rack clashed fast :
And, lo ! a whirlwind hurtled past,
That through the shrinking landscape drave ;
And, yoked with fire and black eclipse,
With dreadful noise besieged the town,
And cast the towers and steeples down,
And roaring seawards smote the ships.
" O God," I cried, "how strong Thy hand !
I see Thy glory, mighty Lord !
The stroke of Thine avenging word,
Nor skies, nor earth, nor seas withstand."
Yet while within my hiding place
I looked on all with troubled glance,
The heaven's most awful countenance
Pierced through the light from the far space
— Where flows its fountain undefiled—

Now swiftly melting, cloud by cloud,
(While breezes echoed not too loud)
Relented everywhere and smiled,
And all the earth was asphodels,
And all the air was fluent gold.
I said unto my heart :—" Behold,
Here is a glory that excels."
And now I read of life and death,
Of sin, and God's sword-bearer, Law,
Until, as in a glass I saw
A face, like His of Nazareth,
All sad as turned toward's Death's goal,
And pale against the stormy skies.
Then round the head began to rise
An arc, like painter's aureole,
Yet clear ; and through that lucent dome,
I saw some hovering cherubim ;
A naked cross on the world's rim ;
And women by an open tomb.
The storm was past, the guerdon won !
And, for the joy before Him set,
That face more marred than any yet,
Was changed, and shone as doth the sun.
I closed the book, and said again :
" Thou art the man that loved me !
Forgiveness surely is with thee ;
And thou canst break sin's fateful chain.'
A still, small voice came from above,
The while I couched even to the dust :—
" *God doth forgive, and yet is just :*
And Law is servant unto Love."

GETHSEMANE.

THE Master after supper went,
In sorrowful bewilderment,
And took with Him disciples three,
To pray in dark Gethsemane.
    High on her hills Jerusalem
    Pallid appeared, while each tree stem,
    Each branch, with dusky blazonry,
    Barred all her moonlit masonry.

He kneeleth in the dim woodland :
The olive trees all listening stand ;
For sorrow's self it seems to be
That weeps, in dark Gethsemane.
    Their plumes the powers of darkness preen,
    And stretch their wings above the scene :
    Shadow on shadow sullenly
    Bends to behold that agony.

'Tis not the moaning of the wind :
It is the mourning of His mind :
O what is dropping fearfully
This hour in dark Gethsemane ?
    God only knows God's sorrow, friends !
    Ye know no plummet that descends
    To sound that deep ! We skim the sea—
    Below, the abyss of mystery !

K

O Peter, eager heart!   Canst thou
Not watch one hour with Jesus now ?
And you, twin souls in truth ! do ye
Too fail in dark Gethsemane ?

    In that dread hour beset, dismayed,
    He turned and saw the murky shade
    Divided, flamewise, slenderly,
    Where watched one angel tenderly.

The Lamb unto the slaughter goes :
The Dove is snared, and plucked the Rose ;
The snake, enwound about life's tree,
Hisses in dark Gethsemane.

    It was the hour of their power.   Came
    No legions, with their swords of flame,
    To guard Him then.   Alone must He
    The winepress tread, for you and me.

MOLOCH.

1.

Men and women of our England
   Have you heard it ?—What is done
To the nestlings and the fledglings
   From the rise to set of sun ?

2.

Have you heard the dreadful rumour
   Of the covenant with death ?
Fathers, mothers, grudge their children
   Even simple vital breath !

3.

Sure primeval man was kinder
   When he framed his bridal bower,
In a seacave, or a hollow
   Of the forest, 'mid the flower

4.

Of the larches, and the bracken—
   Lived and laughed and loved the sun,
Got him sons and got him daughters,
   Careless may be of each one.

K 2

5.

Now the young thing in its voyage
    Reaching earth with wonder mild—
Ghoul meets ghoul and barters grimly
    For the body of the child.

6.

Used by such are sacred titles
    With their meaning all reversed,
Names sublime and symbols holy,
    Flattened down to sense accursed !

7.

Mother, father !   *Trull and bully !*
    Son and daughter !   *Slave and thrall*
Baby love-links—Life's beginning !
    Lust's invested capital !

8.

Sad young pilgrims in the twilight
    'Twixt one darkness and the next !
Daily loom on them the phantoms,
    That we only see perplext

9.

In our dreams, and wake to scorn them ;
    But they shape unto their view
Apish, wolfish, diabolic,
    And *they* know that they are true !

10.

Yea the children have their being
In the terror—crouch within
Till a form shall bulk the doorway
In a reek of fog and gin,

11.

Take and cast them into Torture's
Inner circle of despair.
Thus they live in their Gehenna,
And no hope doth enter there !

12.

Or the faces are not drunken ;
But are moulded on a plan,
As of fearful mediation
'Twixt a devil and a man.

13.

Nakedness, starvation, squalor,
Foul miasma, deadly chill !
Wasting fever, leprous ulcer—
All is grist unto their mill.

14.

Marked with whip, with iron branded,
Dwarfed by injuries unknown,
All the young child shadows passing
Cluster round an unseen throne.

15.

There the great World-Christ receives them,
   Calms their panic, sets them free ;
Folds them, soothes them—"Hush my children !
   They have done it unto Me !"

16.

But to us indignant calls He,
   Who presume to bear His name :—
" These my little kindred suffer !
   Mine the wrong, but yours the shame."

NOTE.—*Vide* reports and inquests touching Infant Life Assurance.

THE POACHER.

"Aye, in the lane twixt the chapel and church
    I seed him as plain as my hand here now."
Plain enough that ! we were fishing for perch,
    And his hand held over the westward bow.

Seemed carved of black basalt, knuckle and crease ;
    For the lake brimmed over with vivid sheen,
All saffron and silver, from fleece on fleece
    Of belated clouds, where the sun had been.

" It's twal' year aboot come next easter sin'
    My mate who was fishing off yonder ness
By himsel' in the whishtful dusk, slipped in—
    Five fathom of water there, as I guess.

And a laucal* preacher improved the death
    At th' Methodis' chapel o' Sunday next—
T'auld Body†—' Thou takkest away their breath,
    They die and return to the dust,' his text.

I'd been a harrigant‡ blayguard, ye ken,
    T'auld over my sins like Cat'olic beads ;
But the word o' the Lord gripped hauld o' me then,
    Till I shivered like these here wobbling reeds.

---

* Local.
  † He means that the chapel belonged to the original body of
Wesleyan Methodists.
  ‡ Arrogant.

Aye, aye, but I was a bad un ! "—A pause
    While he puffed his pipe, and put on a bait—
" Says Scriptur' : 'I'll put a hook in his jaws :'
    (Keep t' line taut.   T' perch are getting agate.)

I tell ye I felt the power o' His might
    Drawing me willy or nilly that day,
See, just as I draw this perch up to light—
    Fair felling my pride by His power, I say.

But still for all that, the drinker was there,
    The feyter,* the poacher, ye understand :
So I wrastled on and on, till in prayer
    I seed him go fram me plain as my hand."

In silence the old man handled his gear.
    A twisted and crumpled shadow was he—
A shadow, a voice in the twilight clear
    Talking his mystical language to me.

" That varra night," he went on again,
    " I hard Him say : ' Tell me, what is thy name ?
' Lord, I'm a blayguard ; but save me ! '   Eh then
    T'auld Adam went out fram me like a flame,

And vanished away across the churchyard.
    And I hollaed out, ' t' auld Adam is gone ! '
Like crier in t' market.   All t' village hard :—
    ' An addle-brained drunkard,' says they, ' is yon.'

---

* Fighter.

Aye, 'twas a merricle—aye just to snatch
  A brand out of t' burning and quench, once more !
Eh ?   T'auld Adam fumbles sometimes at the latch ;
  But canna get in.   T' Almighty keeps t' door."

The mere now barred like a sardonyx stone
  Hath dove-coloured margins dim and withdrawn ;
Half spectral our boat seems on the clear zone ;
  Shadows are stretching from hill and from lawn.

Old friend, who would chide and say thou art mad ?
  Or correct with nice dialectical skill ?
Ah not I !—Ex-poacher, ex-most things bad !
  Moss round thy heart-faith with fantasy still !

IN MEMORIAM.

MRS. J. SPENCER JONES, OF LLANDUDNO.

How pure the air that wanders round this hill,
   Surcharged with odours caught from shrub and flower,
And from a thousand small herbs sweeter still,
   That veil the rocks with innocent glamour,
And nestling close in fragrant amity,
Soothe all the austere winds with spicery !

Before us stretched in many a fine-curved line,
   Range after range, each with its variant hue,
The mountains, changeless, changeful, opaline,
   For ever born afresh in colours new ;
Below, the town : the sea, two sides its wall,
Cleft north and south by this rock terminal.

Meet place for poet, painter, this—to mark
   The yellow-crested morn arise, or night
With purple plumes descend ; or in the arc
   Of heaven the quaint clouds watch, perchance now slight
As thistle down, now like a fleet in sail,
Or now in vast fields, furrowed by the gale.

Here you might view all seasons, in the hope
   And labour of their passion, at your ease :—
Red Autumn on yon mountain's ferny slope ;
   Wild Winter in the intervening seas ;
And Spring yet nearer in these firs, that hear
So soon her voice ; then—Summer—everywhere.

'Twas here, remote, she lived, a lady pure ;
   In lowliness, in patience versed, in praise ;
Her task performing alway—to *endure :*
   Yet, with high thoughts of Him whose steadfast gaze
Looked down the vista of all sorrow, still
She whispered "Lo, I come, to do Thy will !"

Even as the longing lark within its cage,
   Joining the concert of the skies the while,
Sings of the sun and air, its heritage ;
   So, in its fleshly prison, meek exile,
The immortal spirit did its part rehearse
In the great anthem of the universe.

" We in this tabernacle," saith the Word,
   " Do groan." The burden of the travailing world ;
The burden of ourselves, alas ! O Lord !—
   Our watch-tower hopes from their high eminence hurled,
Our souls' ideals by the flesh opprest,
Sins, sorrows, set us craving after rest,

In mystic light, that gathered more and more,
   She tarried for the blest enfranchisement :—
" A light that never was on sea or shore."
   The Herald's *sable,* thus with glory blent,
Became all *argent* in that radiancy ;
And *Death was swallowed up in Victory.*

IN MEMORIAM.

LORD TENNYSON.

October, 1892.

So thou, great Englishman art gone !
Hushed is thy voice of various range
That as a harp well played
Murmured of all things ;—wooed
Soft as a flute ; or made
Music as organs deep ;
Or, as a trumpet shrewd,
Pealed keenly on the steep
Of solitary Helicon—
One voice through sixty years of change !

THE VOICE CRYING IN THE WILDERNESS.

I HEARD a voice when darkness fell,
  One voice when all was still ;
But whence it came I could not tell,
  From plain or far-off hill.

The sound, wind-parted, sank and rose
  A murmur, then a word,
As river-music ebbs and flows
  By pool and shallow ford.

Yet one high note amid the strain,
  Amazed, abased, I found ;
It echoed in my heart again—
  Repent was that clear sound.

The night put on her double veil,
  And blotted out the moon :
The voice—now like a mighty gale
  That storms the woods in June,

And sways the whole immense domain
  Between the grass and sky—
Cried to all flesh, imperious strain !
  ' Behold, your God is nigh ! '

'Not yet, O King! Delay!' I cried.
Recall that word of doom!
If Thou appear, who may abide
The day when Thou dost come?'

But when the dawn grew red with hope
Behind dark belts of firs,
And faint mist slowly mounted up,
Like tangled gossamers,

Oh! then it was a gallant voice—
A herald's silver horn—
That said, 'The King *hath* come! Rejoice!
And sing this happy morn!'

'And where, oh, where,' I asked, 'doth He
Hold His high court apart?'
'Nay, He is here—He calleth thee.
I found Him in my heart!.

VERSICLES.

John i., 1—11.

In the beginning was the very Word,
One essence with the Everlasting Lord,

Companion of the primal loneliness,
And Voice of all the heavenly silences.

The antique atoms, framed in æons old,
He with His right hand swept into a mould,

And spake amid the universal war
Of elements : "Be still : Behold a star !"

Then in the dark-eyed hush of storms, behold
Orb after orb trimmed each a lamp of gold.

In the bright sequence of the stellar choirs
The new born earth flashed with prophetic fires.

From form to form the eager spirit ran :
In Him was life—He gave it unto man !

Light too He gave, that showed the arduous way,
Upwards, far upwards, to the gates of day.

O baffling way ! O weary feet that trod,
Through a dim world, that lonely path to God !

From His high watch-tower in the heavenly land
He looked, He pitied, He stretched forth His hand,

He came unto His own, unveiled His face,
Revealed the Father, full of truth and grace.

They knew Him not, nor guessed His wondrous name
Nor held out hands of greeting when He came.

Yet in that darkness rose the Holy Sun
That never shall go down while ages run.

O Light of Life, still rise amid our fears,
And make a glory in the dusk of years !

Yea shine, Belovèd, to the perfect Day,
And Time's full circle stand at noon alway !

THE TWO FACES.

1.

Long watch by her child the mother kept,
   Whilst the sad wind wailed through the winter thorn ;
But unconscious of her the sick boy slept,
   And wandered heart-broken in fancy forlorn.

2.

For shapes of the night came near and said,
   As he traversed a champaign bleak and hoar,
" Thy mother, O child, thy mother is dead !
   And thou art alone on this desolate shore ! "

3.

The child sank down on the ghostly wild,
   And all silent things into sobbing broke—
Together they grieved, the world and the child,
   And echoes on echoes of sorrow awoke.

4.

The far off murmur of this lament
   From the dim wan world where her darling strayed,
As over him body and soul she bent,
   Made the vigilant heartful woman afraid.

L

5.

And hasting to trim her slender lamp,
  She tenderly cried " I am here, my son ! "
And parted the curls from his forehead damp,
  As she kissed him so softly his cheek upon.

6.

The child, thus summoned from those sad dreams,
  Saw a star grow out of a hollow place ;
Till, behold, lit up by the lamp's faint beams,
  In the half-gloom above him, his mother's face !

" *Give the light of the knowledge of the glory of God in the Face of Jesus Christ.*"

A HYMN.

1.

O GREAT Lord Christ, my Saviour,
    Thou art gone forth to war !
The powers of darkness throng Thee,
    Thou bright and morning Star !
I hear Thy clear voice ringing
    Above the eager fight :—
"Come hither, son, and serve Me,
    And wield the arms of light."

2.

I see amid the darkness,
    Where tides of battle toss,
Aloft Thy broad white banner,
    Marked with the blood-red cross !
And all around are marshalled
    The men whose hearts are pure :
Through Thy anointing Spirit
    They shall, O Christ, endure.

3.

But I am all unstable
    As a wind-shaken reed !
Forgotten vow, and failure,
    And sins, my way impede.

Behold they are as scarlet
    Before Thy Holy Face!
I cannot tell their number :—
    I can but trust Thy grace.

4.

Yet would I, Lord, press near Thee,
    And share Thy toil divine :—
Thy love's long patient vigil,
    Ere lights of morning shine.
My Captain, O my Captain,
    Stretch forth Thy nail-pierced hand,
And claim me by that token
    One of Thy soldier band!

HOMEWARD.

1.

The hard ground echoes to our feet !
   The wind blows straight from the north star
   And glancing from the darkness far
Fall diamond chips of frozen sleet !

2.

Hills tower in their dark solitudes !
   A skirting pinewood on us frowns,
   Shaking its stormy jasper crowns ;
But yet a tender shade secludes !

3.

Where on the hilly terraces
   The ruddy pine stems space the scene,
   And glimmering lights that fall between
Allure the eye with fantasies.

4.

We scarce should wonder now to see,
   Threading with light each woodland aisle,
   A troop of seemly angels file,
With eyes down droopt in piety.

5.

But far away we view outlined,
　　Drawn by the fancy, artist deft,
　　A certain house at sunset left;
Two hands that lift a window blind;

6.

Two eyes that peer behind the pane,
　　And scan the weather for our fate
　　With wonder—will my love be late ?
As now we face the road again,

7.

That onward sweeps with ghostly line
　　Across brown moor and citron hill,
　　Through darkened thorpe, and hamlet still,
By farm, and byre, and hostel sign.

8.

And not to right or left we swerve ;
　　The heart's ideals thrill the blood,
　　And bear us onward like a flood ;
Until at length the well-known curve,

9.

And there below, i' the dimness vast,
　　A red, red core—one dear hearth fire !
　　Ah 'tis the goal of our desire—
O wistful love, I come at last !

A BRUISED REED.

The Master of all music found
　　A bruisèd reed* upon the way :
He breathed its broken orbit round,
　　And woke a song of endless day.

The sweet sound went upon the wind,
　　And thrilled the shepherd on the moor ;
The ploughman paused his team behind,
　　The housewife at the cottage door ;

The hunter listened on the hill,
　　The soldier marching to his doom,
The anxious sailor tossing still,
　　The miner delving in the gloom.

And yet more lovely rang the notes,
　　More pure and true, the high and low,
Until men sighed and said, "There floats
　　Some message to God's world below."

For, subtly changed, that organ rude,
　　By touch and breath that through it went,
Was natured to a finer mood,
　　And wrought a perfect instrument,

---

* According to an ancient interpretation, the " bruised reed " is
the shepherd's rustic flute, marred either in the making or the using.

Whereon the strains he listed he
    Might play alike to age and youth,
And govern all the minstrelsy
    To some surrender of the truth.

And may I bring for thy great use
    This faltering speech—my bruisëd reed ?
Wilt Thou possess, attune, educe,
    O Thou that art the Truth indeed ?